Mary Margaret

and the

Perfect Pet Plan

D1370631

Mary Margaret

and the Perfect Pet Plan

by Christine Kole MacLean

SCHOLASTIC INC.

New York Toronto London Auckland Sydney
Mexico City New Delhi Hong Kong Buenos Aires

To Brad (ahh-choo!), with love and gratitude

ISBN 0-439-86412-7

12 11 10 9 8 7 6 5 4 3 2   6 7 8 9 10 11/0

Printed in the U.S.A.   40

First Scholastic printing, April 2006

Designed by Irene Vandervoort

Acknowledgments

First and foremost, I'd like to thank Stephanie Owens Lurie, who saw that Mary Margaret deserved a bigger canvas than I had given her, and Carla Vissers, who always said the right things as I worked to fill that canvas. Lori Notier and Bill and Michelle Bryson gave me a crash course on middle-school boys; without them I would have been lost.

Over time, Lois Maassen, Mary Peters, Jill Chambers, and Todd Pitock have each helped me take my writing seriously, and—other than their friendship—there is no greater gift they could have given me. Recently, Hope Vestergaard taught me to snort, a skill that's underrated in writing and in life. I owe a special thanks to my corporate clients, especially Kay Scott, Dick Holm, and Randy Braaksma, for understanding that even fiction writers have to put bread on the table.

Finally, I am grateful to Wendie Gerber for marching up to me on the Daisy Brook Elementary School playground on the first day of school and asking me my name. When I told her, she replied:

Christopher Columbus,
What do you think of that?
A big fat lady
Sat upon my hat.
My hat was broke,
And that's no joke!

She then declared, "Now we're friends." And so we were. And so we always will be.

Contents

Contents

Mary Margaret

and the

Perfect Pet Plan

1. Lester on the Loose

The hole in the cardboard box is a bad sign. It looks teeny from my doorway, where I'm standing. But the closer I get to the box, the bigger that hole looks. By the time I'm halfway across the room, I know I'm too late. I know there's a rat loose somewhere in my house.

I've only known Lester for an hour, but if he chewed his way out of the box already, he must be the smartest rat in the world. My dad would say he's an overachiever. My mom would say . . . My mom would say, "WHAT? There's a WHAT loose in my house?" She is the boss of our house. She is also forty-one years old and pregnant, which means that she has not been in the best mood lately.

It's not my fault—about Lester, I mean. (Although her bad mood isn't my fault, either.) I was coming home from the park, making up poems.

Sidewalk, sidewalk,
Don't you wish that you could talk?

Dogs poop on you.
Don't they know about the loo?

My brother, JT, told me *loo* is the way they say *bathroom* in England.

Anyway, I had just finished that poem and was munching some raisins when I saw a pinkish rock that was kind of sparkly. I squatted down to look at it and suddenly Lester was there, right by the rock. I didn't move. He looked up at me with those tiny red eyes and twitching whiskers and I loved him right then. He sat up, sniffed at the last few raisins in my hand, then crawled into my palm and started chowing down. "You sure are a good eater," I told him. I looked around for his owner, but I didn't see anybody. So I brought him home and put him in a cardboard box until I could think of what to do with him.

No, my mom is not going to like this at all. She'll say, "Why, Mary Margaret? *Why* did you bring a rat into my house? I don't care if he is tame!"

And I'll say, "I couldn't just leave him there!"

Then she'll say, "That's not a very good reason."

My mother always wants a good reason for everything. I could be attacked by a lion on the sidewalk and yell "HELP!" in my scaredest voice. And I bet my mother would say, "Give me one good reason." I'm not kidding.

It seems like there's only one reason that my mom thinks is good, and that is "I think I have to throw up." I learned that last summer on the way home from the fair.

My mother isn't big on junk food, so I don't get it very often. But she was in a really good mood that day because she had just quit her job to start her own company. She says that means that now she's not only our boss, but also her own boss. She works from home. The good news about that is I get to see her more, but the bad news is I have to be quiet when she's on the phone, which is all the time.

Anyway, quitting her job put her in such a good mood that she let me buy orange soda, a corn dog, cheesy fries, and cotton candy. For a while I was in heaven! I ate every bit of everything, even though I was full after the corn dog and really full after the cheesy fries. But I went ahead and ate the cotton candy because cotton candy disappears in your spit and never makes it to your stomach at all, so there's always room for cotton candy.

After that we piled into the minivan. I sat in the way back, where it's bumpiest, and JT and his best friend, Duff, sat in the bucket seats in front of me. We took a different road home than we usually do, and on the way we went past some horses. "Can we stop?" I asked, because I always ask whenever we see horses. I like to kiss their soft noses, when they let me.

Mom was driving, like she always does. Everyone in the family knows that she's a better driver than my dad—even my dad. "I'm sorry, but no," she said.

The road was curvy like a snake and hilly like a caravan of camel humps. The car was going up and down and back and forth. Up and down. Back and forth. Up. Down. Back.

Forth. Then my stomach went up. It stayed there, but the car went down.

"Can we stop?" I asked again.

"I don't see any horses," my mom said to my dad. "Do you see horses?"

"No," he said.

That's because there weren't any horses. I didn't feel good. I felt really sick, actually, like I was going to throw up. I leaned forward so I could tell Mom and Dad why I wanted to pull over, but I don't think leaning forward was a good idea because right then I threw up. The good news is I did not throw up on my new leopard-print shorts or my favorite red stretchy shirt with the purple squares. I didn't even throw up on Gary, the toy dinosaur I've had forever. The bad news is I threw up all over the cyber-ranger that JT had won at the fair. It took him about a bazillion tries and his whole allowance plus some of Duff's money to win it. For a minute it looked like he was going to get mad, but then he called it a barf-ranger and laughed.

That is how I know "I have to throw up" is a good reason, and next time that I have to throw up I should say so—right away. When I was little, "I have to go to the bathroom" was a good reason, but it's not anymore.

I wish I could get my mom to understand about this. What I mean is, I didn't mean to bring a rat home. Lester asked me to bring him home—maybe not with words, but he *did* ask—and I couldn't just leave him there. And it's not my fault he chewed his way out of the box. He did that because he's the smartest and strongest rat in the world—and he got that way before I even met him. So none of this is exactly my fault. But there's a good chance Mom won't have the same opinion.

That's why I need to find Lester in the immediate future. I drop to my knees and scramble around my room. I think I see him under the bed, but it turns out to be wadded-up underwear (dirty or clean? Can't tell, don't care) next to a balled-up sock, plus some dust. He's not in the closet or under my pile of dirty clothes or even under my pile of clean clothes.

I try to do what my mom is always telling me to do—put myself in other people's shoes. I close my eyes and think, If I were the world's smartest rat, where would I hide? Then I know! There's still some old butterscotch candies in the Aztec sun piñata that I made for our spring festival, and that's where I would be if I were the world's smartest rat. But either he's not the world's smartest rat or I'm not that good at putting myself into a rat's shoes, because he's not there. I can't find him anywhere.

Unfortunately, I'm pretty sure my mom will be able to. Even when nobody else in the family can find something, she can—even in my messy room. She's scary that way, like a snake that can find its prey by sticking out its tongue. I've watched her to try to see how she does it, and I haven't been able to figure it out. She doesn't use her tongue that I can see, but she has her ways.

"Tch-tch-tch," I say, patting the floor. "Here, boy, here,

boy. Things will be better for you if I find you before my mother does." But either he's not in my room, or he isn't trained to come when he's called. I'll have to take care of that when I find him.

I run out of my room, past JT's room, where JT and Duff are doing homework. When I get to the phone at the end of the hall, I dial my new friend Andy's number.

"Hey, Andy," I say, trying to sound normal. "This is Mary Margaret. Remember? From yesterday? Want to come over?"

"I'd like to," says Andy. "But I'm kind of busy."

"With what?"

"First I was practicing my violin, but right now I'm organizing my sheet music. It got all mixed up during the move."

Organizing music? I guess I still have a lot to learn about Andy. I'd like to yell, "SHEET MUSIC? WHO CARES ABOUT SHEET MUSIC! I'VE GOT A RAT LOOSE HERE!" But JT's door is open so I'm trying to be normal, pretending like I'm having a boring conversation with Andy. "Really?"

JT comes out of his room, walking with one arm crooked out in front of him like a big *Z* and the other arm crooked out behind him. He's trying to walk like an Egyptian. Don't ask me why. He's just weird sometimes. He looks at me out of the corner of his eye. I fake a smile but only because I want him to G.A., which is code for *go away*. He does, down the hall toward the bathroom.

"Yeah. I need to do that before I go meet my new violin teacher in a few minutes."

"Umm-hmm." I listen for the click of the lock on the bathroom door. When I hear it, I cup my hand over my mouth and the receiver. "Look," I say quietly. "You want to be best friends, right?"

"I don't know. I guess."

"Then you need to come NOW. Because that's what best friends do."

"Why now?"

"Because there's a *rat* on the *run* here and I need your help finding it."

"A rat? That's dangerous. You better tell your parents so they can set a trap or put out poison or something."

"No! He's a tame rat."

"How do you know?"

"Because he followed me home from the park."

"Rats don't follow people."

"That's what I mean! He's a tame rat. He wanted me to pick him up."

"Who does it belong to?"

"I don't know. And it's not an *it*. It's a *him*."

"Have you told your mom?"

I slump against the wall. "No. I was going to ask if I could have a pet first."

"I didn't know you wanted a pet."

"Well, I do. And it was perfect that Lester followed me home."

"The rat *and* a guy named Lester followed you home?"

"No! The rat's name is Lester."

"How do you know?"

I clunk my forehead against the wall. "Because I named him Lester!" I say, forgetting to be quiet right then.

I hear the floorboard squeak behind me. "Who's Lester?" asks JT.

I jerk my head up. "Oh . . . uh . . . just a pretend friend!" I say.

"I should have guessed, Imaginary Mary," he says.

Normally I would shoot back, "My name is *Mary Margaret*." And normally he would say what he always says, "That's an awfully big name. You have to grow into a name like that." But I just give a little pretend laugh so he'll leave me alone and go back to his room, which he does.

Andy says, "If I was you, I never would have let that rat in the house."

"But you're not me."

"That's for sure. I wouldn't be you if you gave me all the candy in the world. Or for all the money in the world. Or even for—"

"Okay, okay!" I interrupt. "You don't want to be me."

"You can say that again."

"You don't have to be me! Just come over and help me."

"I can't."

"Because of your dumb sheet music?"

"No. I told you. Because I have to meet my new violin teacher. But even if I didn't, I couldn't come."

"Why not?"

"For one thing, my mom wouldn't let me. Rats have too many germs. And for another thing . . ."

"What?"

"I wouldn't know what tie to wear."

2. Itzy (and Andy)

Here's the deal. I have a pretty good life. Or at least I thought I did, until recently. What I mean is, I have my own library card, clothes that are just right for me, and I'm pretty smart for my age (eight and a half). I also have a scooter and now this new friend, Andy, who apparently likes to wear neckties and worries about germs but is otherwise okay so far. I didn't actually need a new friend until recently, but that's another story. *That* story is about how my mother and I were very attached to each other, but ever since she started expecting a baby it seems like she is way less attached to me than she used to be. Which is why I need a new friend.

Andy and his parents moved to a house behind us a few weeks ago. I can see his backyard from our kitchen table. There's a great jungle gym in that yard—brand-new, with a climbing rope and fireman's pole. That jungle gym goes to waste, though, because the only playing Andy does in that backyard is playing the violin. He practices while he walks around the yard—whole entire songs straight through without stopping.

Ever since they moved in back there, my mom keeps trying to get me to be his friend. It used to be that whenever I'd ask my mom if she wanted to look for bugs with me or hit some tennis balls, she'd say, "Let's go!" But now she says, "Why don't you ask that Andy to play?"

"He doesn't even use his jungle gym," I say. "What would we play?"

And if JT is there, he says, "A duet." He really cracks himself up.

But then a few days ago, I heard Andy out there practicing, then stopping, then playing a little more and stopping. I went to the window to see what was the matter because Andy never stops in the middle of a song. I saw him sitting with a puppy in his lap. The puppy was licking Andy's face and Andy was laughing and holding the violin and bow up high over his head. The puppy kept trying to reach it. Then the puppy would calm down for a minute and Andy would try to play a little more of the song, but the puppy would jump up and nip at the violin. Finally Andy put the violin in its case and just played with the puppy.

After a while, Andy stretched out in the sun on the lawn, and the puppy sprawled out on Andy's chest. I wondered, What does that feel like? Having a puppy on your chest, snuggled up under your chin? Would you be able to feel his heartbeat? I thought about how that puppy didn't leave

Andy alone, not even for a second. It was always right there. I sat very still and very quiet because I was waiting for a thought. When it came, the thought was: Andy won't ever be lonely.

I decided two things right then. One, I wanted what Andy had. Two, until I could get it, Andy would be my friend.

So yesterday after school I went over. He answered the door. He was wearing a striped tie like the one my dad wears to meetings. "Hi," I said. "I've seen you in your backyard, playing the violin."

"Oh." He tugged on his tie. "I like to practice out there." He stood there looking at me like he was trying to decide what I wanted.

I stared right back at him. Didn't he know he was supposed to invite me in? Ask me if I wanted lemonade? Show me his dog? Didn't he know *anything?*

I gave a hint. "You could invite me in. If you wanted."

"Why?"

"To see your stuff. Like maybe you have something interesting in there?" I took a step toward him and looked over his shoulder into the house.

He took a small step back. "Well, I guess I could show you my violin," he said.

"Or maybe a dog?" I took another step. Andy backed into the hall.

"Oh, Itzy? That's what I named him. He's my good-sport present. I got him for being a good sport about moving here." Andy shrugged. "You want to see him?"

By then, I was already two steps past him, calling, "Here, Itzy! Here, boy!"

So that is how just yesterday Itzy got to be my friend. And Andy, too, of course.

...spent porc...I yell...when being...and gri...tind nike-
ing here...since...changed. "You were...see him...
...are already...my...hand from...stilbe...

3. My Name Is Mary Margaret!

I look for Lester for a while longer but finally give up and head downstairs.

Duff is at the bottom of the stairs, getting ready to leave. "Why do you have to go already?" JT says to him. "We aren't even done with the map yet."

"I got some other stuff going. You finish it, JT," Duff says, pulling on his jacket. "You're better at it anyway." He opens the door, then stops. "Almost forgot my ball," he says. "It's over there. Toss it to me?"

Without saying anything, JT scoops up the basketball and passes it to Duff.

"Bye, Duff," I say, starting to sit down on the couch.

"Hey! Watch out for Lester!" Duff yells.

I leap up and away from the couch. "Where?" I say, forgetting that he doesn't know that Lester is a rat.

"Oh, man! You almost sat on him!" Duff says. "That's the thing about invisible friends. You can't see them!" I can hear him hardy-har-har-ing as he leaves.

"Ha, ha, ha," I say. JT scuffs into the living room and plops down at the computer. He doesn't even rub the joke in, which is not normal. But there are bigger things on my mind—and in my house.

The whole time I was looking for Lester I was also thinking about what I was going to tell my mother. Even when she's in a good mood, she doesn't like anything that scurries. But maybe if I start out talking about something more normal, like a cuddly kitten or spunky puppy—everyone loves those—then maybe she'll get used to the idea of a pet. And maybe once she's used to the idea of a pet, then maybe she could get used to the idea of a rat.

I watch her, sitting at the other end of the couch, folding tiny T-shirts. They look like they would be just the right size for a cat. "Mom," I say. "Can I have a pet?"

"Oh, I don't know. Maybe someday," she says.

"I was thinking maybe soon-ish."

"How soon-ish?"

"Not today. I know it would take some time to find the right one." Especially, I think to myself, when the right one is loose and hiding from me. "Maybe next week?"

"I don't know, Mary Margaret. There's so much else going on. Why do you want a pet?"

"I just do."

"That's not a very good reason."

Good reasons are hard to find, but I do my best. "That new boy, Andy—the one who lives behind us? He has a pet."

"If Andy jumped off a cliff, would you do it, too?"

JT looks up from his computer. "Why would Andy jump off a cliff?"

"JT, you know what I'm trying to say, but I'm not sure Mary Margaret does." Mom picks up two big yellow cotton balls—at least that's what they look like to me. But then she says, "Look at these tiny socks. I still can't believe there will be another baby in the house!"

There will not actually be a baby in this house for months and months—not until after my birthday. And whenever I talk about my birthday, my mom says, "There's no reason to talk about that yet. It's months and months away." So as far as I'm concerned, there is definitely no reason to talk about that baby yet.

"I know what you're trying to say," I say to my mom.

"Hmm?" she says, smoothing the socks out on her lap.

I pick up a pair of my jeans from the clean laundry pile and hand them to her so she can fold them. "I know what you're trying to say. About getting a pet. I don't get one just because everyone else does."

"That's right." She hands my jeans back to me. "Here, *you* fold these."

"No, I can't. Not neat like you."

"Just do the best you can." I quickly do it because if I don't, she'll start telling me how to fold laundry, which means we won't be talking about my getting a pet.

My mother glances at the folded ball of pants and says, "I'm not sure you're ready for a pet. And I'm pretty sure that I'm not."

"You don't have to be ready for it, because I would take care of it." And I honestly will—just as soon as I find it.

"That's what I'm not sure about. Sometimes you're not very responsible—like just now with these pants. I know you can do better, but you don't try. You want me to do it for you."

"I could have told you that a long time ago," says JT.

"Oh, hush," she says to him.

"It's true, though. You baby her, Mom."

Mom says to me, "It is partly my fault. I have always thought of you as my baby, just because you're the youngest. You're eight—"

"Almost nine," I say. "Old enough to get a pet."

"It's not a matter of being old enough. You need to be *big* enough. You need to be big inside."

"Puh-lease, Mama," which is what I used to call her all the time and what I call her now when we snuggle. "Please. A pet would help me be big inside."

She looks at me and sighs. She is a big sigher. "I'll think about it," she says.

JT says that means probably not. "You might have better luck if you wait a while, Small Fry."

"My name is Mary Margaret," I say. "Not Small Fry."

He doesn't say anything. He doesn't have to. Even if he isn't saying it out loud, he's thinking it: Mary Margaret is a big name. You have to grow into a name like that.

JT grew into his name a long time ago, which is pretty easy to do when your name only has two letters. He's not bad for a big brother, I guess. He just turned thirteen. He gets to ride his bike where he wants during the day and he gets to use the Internet all by himself. He hangs around the house a lot, even though Mom is always telling him to get some fresh air or see some friends.

But he says he likes it at home. He says kids his age aren't that interesting. Mostly all they do is skateboard and hang out at the mall or watch TV, and he'd rather be on the computer. Duff used to be here all the time and they played computer games or baked terrific cookies. My mom calls JT and Duff "Velcro buds" because they always stick together, but maybe their Velcro is wearing out, because Duff hasn't been around much lately and the only thing in the cookie jar right now is crumbs.

JT has his own room, which is way more interesting than mine and which I am supposed to stay out of. When I don't, JT yells at me, but Mom just says, "I expect more of you, Mary Margaret." I hate it when she says that.

JT also has his own Web site, jtcity.com, and anybody who goes to his site can help him build a pretend city. He's had it for a long time, but only eighty-two visitors have been to the site—and that includes all the times he's been there. He let me go there once and I built a school, but I built it on a swamp. As we watched the school sink into the swamp, JT said that I should remind him never to live in a city where I'm the city planner. When the tippy-top of the flagpole finally disappeared into the muck, I said, "I knew that would happen." Even though I said it like I meant it, he didn't believe me. Besides being lucky, JT is also smart, but I'd never tell him so.

Did I say that he gets to stay up until ten o'clock at night? *His* life already *is* perfect.

4. Do Rats Have Dander?

At dinnertime, without being asked, I set the table. It isn't really my thing—it's too dishy, if you ask me—but I do it anyway because I know Mom is still thinking about getting a pet. At least she is supposed to be, but I can never be sure she hasn't forgotten. She forgets important stuff like this all the time now. She says it's the baby.

Maybe it is the baby, but to me it sounds like the same old trick my neighbor, Jolene, uses when she does something wrong. She always says her invisible friend, Lucy, did it. Last year Jolene colored her brand-new Easter dress with permanent markers and blamed it on Lucy, which isn't even that smart. Why would Lucy, *who is invisible,* color on Jolene's *real* dress instead of on her own invisible dress? Jolene is only five and spoiled, so she can get away with stuff like that. But my mom? I expect more of her.

My dad is working late, so it's just the three of us, which means there should be plenty of time to talk about what I want to talk about. All through dinner I wait for my mom to remember about the pet. I wait through the lettuce salad and the pea soup and the pork chops and rice. I wait through soggy beans and a second glass of milk. I wait through the dumb joke that JT made up. ("What do you call a cat that has a computer? Chip-purr. Get it? Chip—like a computer chip. Purr—cats purr when they're happy. Chipper!") I even wait through dessert, which isn't that hard to do since I love carrot cake, which has two of my favorite things in it—carrots and cake. But by the time I'm helping Mom do dishes, all my patience for waiting is worn out. I take a deep breath and tell myself, Do not whine. If there's one thing my mother cannot stand, it's whining.

"I would really like a pet," I say, without whining even a little. "A cat would be nice." My friend Justin has a cat and he says he's teaching it karate. I wouldn't care if my cat didn't know karate. I would be happy with an average cat that just lies around.

She takes a plate from me and puts it in the dishwasher. "Not so nice for Daddy," she says. "Cats have dander."

"What's that?"

"Tiny pieces of animal skin, kind of like dandruff. It makes Daddy sick."

I love my dad, but I really want a pet. "How sick? Throw-up sick or sniffle sick?"

"Very sick. He's highly allergic, Mary Margaret. We can't have a cat." She looks around the kitchen. "Hand me that pan, would you?"

The pan still has some pea soup in it. I think a better

name for pea soup would be pea slop, but I don't say so. Instead, I hand it to her very carefully and hope she notices how grown-up I am being.

"How about a dog?" My Aunt Wendie has a dog named Pearl. She's twenty-one years old, but she's still only a puppy because dogs count years different than people do. She has a bright pink leash and a collar with sparkles on it. I'd be happy with just a plain brown collar and leash as long as there was a dog on the other end.

"Dogs have dander, too," she says.

"A chipmunk?"

"Dander. Anything with fur has dander."

"How about a horse?" My sitter, Jamie, has a horse named Forest. He is the neatest horse ever born because he has one blue eye and one brown eye, but I would be totally happy with an ordinary horse that had two eyes the same color.

"No place to keep it. And horses also have dander."

"But horses don't have fur. They have hair."

Mom drops the silverware into the sink with clatter. "Anything that has *fur* OR *hair* has dander."

Suddenly I remember that there already is something with fur or hair in this house. "What about rats? Do they—"

"YES, rats do! And so do guinea pigs, hamsters, and hedgehogs!"

It wasn't very nice of my mother to interrupt, but I don't say so. I won't say one more word about pets until after the baby is born. Maybe by then she'll be less crabby. Maybe I won't say one more word to her at all *about anything* until after the baby is born.

I leave without helping her finish the dishes, and she lets me get away with it. I hide out in my room and think about how Lester is very small and how much dander could a little rat like him have, anyway? And why does my mom have to be so mean about everything? It used to be that after dinner we'd do tickle time or play a game of checkers. But now she's just *blah*. It's not fair that she's blah. I didn't ask her to have a baby. Nobody even asked me what I thought about adding another person to our family. And if she has to be *blah*, she could at least get me a pet. But then I think that I kind of already have one—Lester—only no one knows about him except Andy. So after I find him, maybe Lester can just keep on being my secret pet. No one knows about him now and things are going okay, so why not? And that idea cheers me up quite a bit.

When my dad gets home from working late, he stops by my room. "Hello, Mary Margaret," he says. "How was your day?"

I'm extra glad to see him tonight, and I give him a bear hug around his waist.

"Ugh!" he says. "You're squeezing my guts out." But I don't stop for another minute because I know that I'm not really squeezing his guts out and I like the way he smells like grass. That's how he always smells, even in winter and even though he works in an office where his job is to go to meetings and keep everyone happy. He wears a baseball cap most of the time. He says that's because he has less hair than he used to, so he has to wear it to keep his head warm.

When I finally let go, he sits down on the floor. "So-o-o," he says. He tugs on the front of his cap and smiles at me. "Want to help me warm up my thinking cap?"

"I'm too old for that," I say.

"Well, I'm not! Come on. Do it for your dad."

So I tug the cap two times quick. It's a silly game that me and him made up when I was a little kid. To tell the truth, I don't like to play it that much anymore, but he still does. So maybe it's a good thing Mom's having a baby, because when it grows up a little that baby will be able to play the game.

"I understand you want a dog," my dad says.

"Yeah," I say. "Or a cat. A cat would be good."

"I like dogs, too."

"Really?"

He nods. "Really. But just like Mom said, I'm allergic. When I'm in a house where dogs or cats live, right away the dander makes it hard for me to breathe. I start sneezing— achoo, achooo, AHHHHH-CHOOOO!—and I can't stop. My eyes water so much that it looks like I'm crying over nothing." He puts his arm around me. "It's a little embarrassing for a big guy like me. Crying over nothing."

"So it's like Mom when she cuts onions?"

"Kind of like that. So I—wait. Now I really *do* have to sneeze." He covers his mouth and sneezes two little sneezes in a row. "Sorry about that. I must be coming down with a cold. Where was I? Oh, yes. So I can't live in a house with those kinds of pets."

"Oh," I say. "I wish you didn't have allergies."

"Me, too. I'm sorry about that."

"I know. It's okay, I guess."

He puts his finger on my chin and turns my face toward his. "You sure? Because I could just move out. We could get a doghouse, and I could live in the doghouse, and the dog could live here." My dad's a big joker.

"No," I say. "Mom wouldn't like sleeping in the same bed with a dog."

"There won't be room for a dog in that bed for much longer, anyway."

"Why not?"

He points to his stomach. "Pretty soon Mom's going to be as big as a pumpkin. I don't think the bed is big enough for her, a pumpkin, and a dog. Do you?"

"Da-ad," I say, trying not to smile. "Stop fooling around."

He turns his cap around backward so that we can hug.

"How do you feel about rats?" I ask.

"Rats? Give me a minute." He stares at the ceiling for about a second. "Nope. Not that fond of them, actually," he says.

"Well, maybe we can find another kind of pet," I say. "One that doesn't have dander, like a salamander or fish? Fish don't have dandruff, do they?"

"I don't think so. That's not a bad idea. But your mom has a lot on her mind right now. She's trying to finish up a big project for one of her customers, and she's thinking a lot about the baby."

"So?"

My dad twists his cap around and tugs on it himself. "So she feels like she can't think about one more thing right now."

"Humph," I say. "Two things. That doesn't sound like so much to me."

"Having a baby is a big deal."

"I don't know why," I say. "I've seen babies. They're little. Besides, there will still be you and me and Mom and JT. We'll still live here. Things won't really change, right?"

"Well, no—and yes," he says. "There will be all of us, plus one. We'll be adding a new member to the family. And no, we won't be moving to a new house. But we will have to make some adjustments and make some room."

I think about this. There's plenty of room in the minivan and we already have six chairs around the kitchen table, so there's no problem there. We do only have three bedrooms, though. "Oh! Like we're going to make Mom's office into the baby's room," I say.

"We might someday," he says, "but not right away."

"But a pet could stay right in my room. We wouldn't even have to make room for a pet." And then I think of Lester and add, "In fact, I bet you wouldn't even know that there's one here."

My dad sighs. "Don't push it right now. Just give your mom some time." Dad holds up one finger, waits, waits,

waits, and then—"Ahhhh-CHOOOO!"—sneezes. I hand him a Kleenex and he wipes his eyes, which have started to water. "Boy, I'd better start taking my vitamins and try to get rid of this thing before it gets worse. Wow! It almost feels like allergies, though."

Suddenly I'm thinking that maybe Lester already is in my room, after all. If Lester is in my room, it's time to get Dad *out* of my room. "Uh, Dad, are you hungry?" I ask, as I get up and walk toward the door. "How about a nice sandwich?"

"A little hungry," he says, following me. "But isn't that strange? Now I'm getting an allergic reaction when I *just talk* about anything with dander!"

"Weird," I say, glancing nervously behind me. I think I hear some skittering on the wood floor over by my window, but I can't be sure. It might just be the branches of the tree outside. Just in case, I close my bedroom door behind me and hope Lester won't be able to squeeze through the gap between the door and the floor.

On the way to the kitchen, I hear the phone ring.

"Dibs!" I yell, racing to the living room to pick it up.

JT gets there first. "I don't think so," he says, holding the receiver up high so I can't reach it.

"JT, give it!"

"Who would be calling you?" he asks.

"Who would be calling *you*?" I ask right back.

"Who is bigger?" he says, and then he says "Hello?" into the phone.

I jump as high as I can, still trying to reach the phone. He gives me a look that means "Stop it or *else*." I give him a look back that means "Who made you king, anyway?"

He turns his back on me. I step up right behind him and pretend I'm his shadow.

"Oh, hi," he says into the phone.

"Oh, hi," I say, copying him. He gives me a dirty look.

"Uh-huh," he says.

"Uh-huh," I say, exactly the way he said it. He turns fast and bumps me off balance with his hip and I fall onto the couch.

"HEY!"

"Quit bugging me," he hisses. Then he says into the phone, "Yeah, I'm still here. Yeah, it was just Mary Me!-Me!-Me-garet. What? Oh . . . okay. Yeah. See ya."

Mom comes in just as he hangs up. "Who was that?" she asks before I can even tell her how JT was bossing me.

"Duff."

"What did he want?"

"Nothing." Normally JT pretends to step on me or trip over me when I'm lying on the floor, like I am now, but he just walks right by.

"Then why did he call?"

"I don't know."

"Weren't you supposed to get together?"

"I guess."

"Are you going to?" she asks.

"Guess not," he says.

"Why not?" I ask, pulling myself up from the floor.

"He's got something else going."

"Again?" Mom says. "It's getting to be a regular thing, him changing plans."

"It's no big deal," JT says.

Mom opens her mouth like she wants to say something, but then she closes it again, and then she opens it again, which makes her look a little like a fish. Finally she says, "I'm going to sit with your father while he has a sandwich. Anyone want to join us?"

"No, thanks," I say.

JT shakes his head and sits back down at the computer.

"What are you doing?" I ask him.

He groans. "Couldn't you just leave me alone right now?"

"I just want to know what you're doing."

"Homework."

"That doesn't look like homework to me," I say. "It looks like you're watching a movie."

"I'm not watching it. I'm making it."

"Can I be in it?"

JT sighs. "Yeah, sure. Why not? I need to do this sometime, anyway. In fact, you have to be in it. I have to do a family tree, but Mr. Bryson said we could make it however we wanted to, so I'm doing mine on the computer. I'm going to use pictures, but I'm going to include video and audio interviews of family members. Which includes you, unfortunately."

"What do I have to do?" I ask.

"Just answer a few questions. That's the easy part. The hard part is that you have to act normal. Be yourself. Think you can do it?"

"N.P.," I say. That's code for "No problem." "I'll go get ready."

"There's nothing to get ready for."

"I can't be myself in this old thing," I say, pulling at my T-shirt. "It will just take a sec." I race back upstairs and pull out my box of very special clothes. I put on the purple paisley dress and white go-go boots my mom gave me when she was cleaning out the attic. She also gave me something called a fall, which is like a wig only it makes your own hair look longer, and I put that on. Then I see my old tiara, and since I'm in a tiara kind of mood, I put that on, too.

I run back downstairs. "Okay, I'm ready," I tell JT, sliding into the chair by the desk.

Just then Mom comes in, looking for the newspaper. "Let me guess," she says to JT when she sees me sitting in front of the camera. "You called her Mary Movie-Star."

JT shakes his head. "No. I told her to be herself."

I put my hand up to my head and lightly touch the tiara. "Is it on straight?" I ask. My mom smiles and nods. "Good. Let's go!"

JT makes sure the camera is in the right place, and then he says, "Just tell me a little about yourself. Ready? And *action!*"

I flip the blonde hair of the wig behind my shoulder and

take a deep breath. "My name is Mary Margaret. I like to do crafts and to color and I like animals. I would really like a pet and my mom said she would think about it. I'm JT's sister and Dave and Lillian's daughter and I live here with all of them. That's my mom standing back there. I don't know if you can see her or not, but she's usually not this fat. She's going to have a baby, but there's no need to talk about that yet. Ummm . . . oh! I like to make up little poems about my life. Like this.

> *"They named me Mary Margaret*
> *And said that I was heaven sent.*
> *So I think that this next baby*
> *Will be a great big acciden—"*

"Cut!" says Mom.

"That'll work," says JT. "Don't worry, Mom. I can edit."

"Add what?" I ask.

"Not add it," he says. "Edit. I can get rid of the stuff I don't like or change it until I do like it." He looks at the computer screen for a minute and taps a few keys. Then he says, "It would be nice if you could do that to life."

I don't get it. He already has a perfect life. So what would he like to change?

5. Visit from the Rat Man

JT might think he has problems, but I *do* have a problem. A real live problem that's still on the loose. My dad has stopped sneezing, but I can hear him sniffling in the other room. When he says, "Come on, Mary Margaret. I'll tuck you in," I know what I have to do.

"That's okay, Dad. You've had a long, hard day at the office, and I'm getting older. I think I'll just tuck myself in."

"What?"

"No, really. I want to."

My dad looks at my mom, who arches one eyebrow at me.

"Remember? You told me I need to be big inside," I say to her.

"That's true, but I didn't mean—"

I give each of them a hug and say, "I know. But I *want* to."

My mom and dad used to take turns tucking me in, but lately it's been my dad because my mom is so *exhausted* (which is her new favorite word) by nighttime. That's why I have to say I'll put myself to bed. I have to save my dad from his allergies.

Because of the way my dad was sneezing in my room, I'm pretty sure that Lester is there. I think maybe the only way to find him is to actually clean my room, which I haven't done in quite a while. My mom would say I have "let things go" in my room, and that was pretty true even before Lester got loose.

I start with the heap of boxes and crayons and paper and glue sticks in one corner because I think he might be there. But he's not, and just cleaning up that pile takes me a lot longer than I thought it would, and I'm too *exhausted* to keep cleaning. So I just make sure my door is closed tight and then I climb into bed. Maybe I'll find him tomorrow.

What I said to my mom and dad about wanting to put myself to bed is not really true. I don't want to read by myself and I feel silly making up a prayer poem without my mom or dad being here to hear it. But out of habit I say, "Bless slimy toads, bless leafy trees, bless squirmy worms, and please bless me."

I used to say the Kiki Blessing every night. My kiki is the blanket I've had since I was a baby. I couldn't say *blankie*, so I always called it my kiki, even when I got better at talking. Anyway, the Kiki Blessing went like this:

God bless my kiki and bless it well.
Never mind that it's ratty,
Never mind that it smells.
Unless I have it, I don't feel right.
God bless my kiki, on this and every night.

A while ago I decided that I was too old for my kiki and so we packed it in a box in my closet. But lately when my dad says, "Sweet dreams" and shuts off my light and leaves my room, I miss that kiki something awful. I especially miss it tonight. One reason is that I hear new noises in my room—scratching and scraping and clicking. It's probably Lester, and even though him and me aren't that familiar yet, sharing my room with him would be okay. This might be the closest I ever come to having a pet.

But I'm not positive it's Lester. It might be something bigger and meaner, with scales and pointy teeth that shoot poisonous venom. And claws that can rip right up through my mattress. And giant lips that can suck me right out of my bed. I'd disappear and no one would ever know.

I used to get scared about stuff like this every night when I was six or seven. My dad would say, "You have an overactive imagination, Mary Margaret. You're scaring yourself." He taught me a bunch of tricks back then, like thinking about the beach or remembering a birthday party. I try them tonight, but nothing is working. Maybe that's because this time there is something *real* scaring me, not just my imagination.

It takes me a long time to fall asleep, and things don't get any better after I do. I dream that the house is full of crawling babies. Each baby is carrying an animal in its mouth and all the babies are crawling out the door, following my mother, who is wearing a pointy cap like the one the Pied Piper wears in that fairy tale. And she's shouting at me, "Mary Margaret! Mary Margaret!" And in my dream

I'm trying to answer her, "What? What?" I don't know why, but she doesn't hear me. She just keeps shouting.

"*Mary Margaret!*"

I wake up with a jerk and look at my clock. It's morning and my mom really is calling to me. I can tell from the *pings* on my window that it's raining and I think, April showers bring May flowers, but it's not April anymore. It's June.

"What?" I say to my mom.

"Andy is here."

"Okay." I put on my bathrobe and pad downstairs, where Andy is waiting. My mom asks him if he would like to stay for breakfast. When he says "No, thanks," she goes back to the kitchen. As soon as she's gone, Andy shoves a crumpled, soggy piece of paper at me. "Look what I saw when I was walking Itzy," he whispers.

There's a picture of Lester and the words:

LOST.

Bridgette.

Friendly, tame, loving white rat with red eyes.

Call 555-6743.

REWARD.

"Well, I wouldn't have been able to keep him—I mean her—anyway," I say. "My dad is really, really allergic."

Andy makes me promise I'll call him and tell him what happens, then goes home. When my parents are getting ready for work, I call the number.

"I saw your poster," I say. "I have Bridgette."

"That's fantastic!" the man says. "Has she had her babies yet?"

"Babies?"

"Yes, she's going to have them any day."

More babies. Hey, maybe Rat Man would give me one of the babies as a reward instead of money! But then I remember, Oh yeah, Dad's allergic.

Rat Man is still waiting for an answer. "Well? Has she had the babies?"

"I'm not sure," I say. "I haven't actually seen her since yesterday afternoon. She's hiding somewhere in my room, I think."

"I'll be right over!" Rat Man says.

"No! My parents don't know she's here, and I'm trying to show them that I'm responsible, because I would like a pet. But if they find out she's here, then it's not going to be so great for that," I blurt out. "Can't you just wait until after school? If you can just wait until four o'clock to come, my parents won't be here then." JT will be, but I'll worry about that later.

"But if she has her babies today—" he says.

"Then you can come and get them all!"

"No, if a human touches the babies in the first few days, the mother might reject them or even kill them," Rat Man says in a don't-argue-with-me voice. "I'm coming over. Now."

The front door of our house is right by the stairway, and the kitchen is way in the back of the house. By the time Rat

Man shows up, my parents are eating breakfast, but JT is still in his room. I open the door before the man can ring the bell, put my finger to my lips, and wave my hand so he'll know to follow me. When we get to my room, Rat Man sits down, lays his hand flat on the floor, and clucks softly, "Bridge-Bridge-Bridge-y, time to go home. I have some nice peanuts for you." Bridgette runs out from under a mound of doll clothes, stops, looks at him, then me, then him. She runs into his hand and starts to munch a peanut.

"I tried that," I say. "Calling her. But I didn't know her real name, so it didn't work."

Rat Man is stroking her belly. "Still pregnant," he says. "But I bet it happens today."

Rat Man gives me the ten-dollar reward and we sneak down the hall—just as JT is coming out his door. "Hey!" he says. "Who are you?"

"JT, shhh!" I say. "It's okay. He found Lester—I mean, Bridgette."

"Wait. Your invisible friend? Come on, Mary Margaret. Get real!"

"No," I hiss. "Lester is a *rat*—loose in my room and then Andy saw a poster—had to get her out right away—Mom and Dad can't know, or I'll *never* get a pet. So please, *please* don't say anything!" When I get nervous, I talk very fast. I get that from my dad.

JT frowns at me for a minute, like he can't understand what I am saying, but then steps back so that me and Rat Man can sneak back down the stairs. He follows us, and when I close the door behind Rat Man, JT crosses his arms and says, "Talk. But talk slow."

So I tell him everything and I get almost all the way done before Mom comes to the stairs, looks around, and then crosses *her* arms. JT must get that arm-crossing thing from her. "*What* is going on?" she says.

For a minute, JT and I just look at her like we've forgotten how to talk. I don't know what to say. Even worse, I don't know what JT will say.

"Who tracked mud up the stairs already this morning?" she says.

Oh, mud. I was so busy telling JT about everything that I didn't even notice that Rat Man tracked in mud.

Mom says, "JT? Those footprints are too big to be Mary Margaret's."

"Uh . . . yeah," JT says. "It was me."

"Well, clean it up, please," she says, shaking her head like she is disappointed in him.

"Sure. Okay."

After Mom goes upstairs, I say, "I'll do it."

"You're right," he says.

"JT?"

"Yeah?"

"Thanks for not telling."

"For not telling *yet*?" he says. "You're welcome."

He's just kidding about that *yet* stuff. At least I think he is.

6. A Not-So-Buggy Strategy

That night after dinner, my mom takes her turn in front of the camera for JT's family tree project. She says, "My name is Lillian Anderson. I'm proud to say that I'm JT's mother, and Mary Margaret's, and soon, the mother of child number . . ."

"Three," I say.

"Thank you, Mary Margaret," she says. "I think I know how many children I have." She turns back to the camera. "I like to spend time with my family, and I also like to read and go biking, although it will be a while before I go biking again." She rubs her tummy. "I work part-time from home. I'm a corporate events planner."

"That means she plans biiiiiig, boring parties," I say, trying to be helpful. "Clowns never come to her parties."

"Cut!" JT says. "Mary Motor Mouth, this is Mom's turn. You had your turn."

"Okay, okay," I say.

"She's right," my mom says to JT. "They are boring if

you're eight years old. Besides, I think I'm finished. Is there anything else you needed me to talk about?"

"No. Most kids are only using photos of their relatives. I just wanted to get everyone saying a little bit to make it more interesting."

Just then the phone rings, and since JT is still talking to Mom, for once I get to it before he does.

It's Andy. "You *said* you'd call me," he says, all mad.

"Sorry. I guess I just forgot."

"You *promised*."

"Well, I *forgot!*" I'm thinking just then that Andy might not be that fun to have as a friend. Itzy is barking in the background, and suddenly I have a good idea. "Why don't I come over and tell you about it now?"

"Okay, and then we can play Battleship."

"And play with Itzy," I say.

I play with Itzy the whole time I am telling Andy about Rat Man and Lester being pregnant and the mud and JT. Andy listens to the whole thing, twisting the end of his red tie around his pointer finger during the really exciting parts.

"Wow. And all that happened before school, huh?" he says, getting Battleship out of the cupboard and starting to set it up.

"Yeah, practically before I was even all the way awake," I say.

"You want the blue set or the red set?" he asks.

"I really should be getting home."

"But you said that you'd play Battleship."

"No, I didn't."

"But it's only fair! We did what you wanted and now it's my turn."

"Technically we did what you wanted, Andy. You're the one who wanted to hear about Rat Man. Besides, how can I concentrate on playing when I'm trying to figure out how to get a pet?"

Andy is quiet for a minute. He opens up the red Battleship station and starts to fiddle with the ships. Then he says, "So that means if I help you figure it out, then we can play."

I shrug.

He bites his lip. "Maybe what you need is a strategy. A plan for how to get a pet. Why won't your mom let you have one?"

"Besides my dad being allergic? I don't know. She says I'm not big enough inside and I need to show her that I am. But that will take forever! Also, my dad says she has a lot on her mind."

"So you have to put this on her mind. But not in a bug-gy way."

"Not in a bug-gy way?"

"Yeah, find a nice way to remind her."

"That is a great idea, Andy, and I know just how I'm going to do it. You're a genius!"

"Really?"

"According to me you are."

Andy's face starts to match his red tie. "That's just what friends do, right? Help each other."

"Right," I say, getting up to leave.

"Hey! What about Battleship?"

"Maybe next time."

I lie awake in bed that night, working on my strategy. My mom loves music and music is not at all bug-gy, which is why I make up a song and sing it to the tune of "Rudolph the Red-Nosed Reindeer." Mom knows the tune, so maybe she'll even sing along once she learns the words.

Ma-a-a-ry Margaret
Really would like a pet.
One that she could take care of,
It would never need the vet.
One that she could teach tricks to
And would keep her company
And love her more than pet food.
A pet would make her so happy!

The next day I start singing it. Often, whenever my mother is around. I sing it quietly all the way to the grocery store. "Catchy tune," my mom says.

I shout it on the way home. "Very nice," she says.

I sing it silly after dinner. She sticks her fingers in her ears.

By Day Two of my musical plan, singing it is such a

habit that I don't even know I'm doing it all the time. I find out I am, though, when we're doing yard work. That's when my mom says, "Enough is enough, Mary Margaret! If you pester me any more about a pet, I'm going to tear my hair out. We simply can't get a pet right now!"

She says it louder than she needs to, if you ask me.

I don't care if I am almost nine. I cover my face with my hands and I start to cry. It's not a fake cry, either. It's big and wet and blubbery and real. I feel like if I don't get a pet to love soon, my heart will dry up like a worm on a hot sidewalk.

All that crying surprises my mom. "Mary Margaret?"

"I can't help it!" I say. "I want a p-p-pet so bad so I can't stop p-p-pestering you. And I don't want you to be b-b-b-b-bald!" I don't say it, but what I would like right this minute is my kiki.

My mom wraps her arms around me, and I let her. "You're all bones and I'm all baby, but somehow we'll manage," she says, as she gives me a big hug. I snuffle into her sleeve and rub my eyes with my muddy hands. She digs a Kleenex out of her pocket and tries to wipe my tears. "If JT were here, he'd call you Muddy Margaret."

That only makes me start crying again.

"I'm sorry," she says. "I shouldn't have said that, should I?"

I shake my head against her chest.

"Listen, Loverly," she says, and as soon as she calls me Loverly, I start to feel better. "I know you want a pet more than anything. I'll try to figure something out. I'll do what I can."

I snuffle some more. "You will?"

I can feel her chin bump against the top of my head when she nods. "Yes, but you will have to be patient and flexible. Can you do that for me?"

"Why do I need to be able to touch my toes before I can get a pet?"

"No, a different kind of flexible," she says. "What I mean is, it might not be what you expect. It might not be what you would normally think of as a pet."

"Sure, sure! I can be flexible. We could start really slow. How about a snake?"

"Hmmmmmmm," she says.

Later when I find JT at the computer and tell him about it, he says that means maybe. "Could be yes, could be no, Squirt. I wouldn't count on her to get you one."

"Why not?"

"Because of the ba—"

"*Bay-beee!*" I finish in a snotty voice.

"Yeah. The baby. Put yourself in Mom's shoes. There hasn't been a baby around here for nine years, and Mom's pretty old to be doing this. A few days ago I heard her crying in her bedroom. When I asked her what was wrong, she said that nothing fit anymore—even her shoes are too small. And then she said she didn't know how she was going to fit everything in, like taking care of the baby and working and everything."

If she can't fit everything in, I wonder, then will I be one of the things she leaves out? I ask JT, "Then what about me?"

"It's not all about YOU, Mary Margaret. You can't be the center of attention forever."

That's not what I meant, but JT doesn't get what I'm trying to say, so I just cross my arms and say, "So?"

"So stop bugging her about it and come up with something that you can do to help her out. KWIM?"

KWIM stands for "Know What I Mean?" but I don't really. He's talking about Mom when what I want to know is, what's going to happen to me?

A while later he says he's going to the library. I ask him if I can watch my part of his family tree movie again.

"Yeah, sure. There it is," he says, and he points to a folder on the screen that has MM on it. "But nothing else, Mini-Margaret. My computer folder where all my files are is just like my room."

"I know, I know," I say. "'No admission without permission.' And it's Mary Margaret."

"It's a big name," he yells over his shoulder as he leaves the house. "If you would grow into it, then I wouldn't have to remind you not to snoop."

When I watch myself this time, I'm not in a tiara mood anymore and I wish I hadn't worn it. It makes me look like I'm a little kid playing dress-up. I wonder if JT would let me do my movie over. I'd ask him if he would just come back from the library, but he is taking a long time.

After I close that file, I see the MOM file. I should probably ask first, but I don't think JT would mind if I watched Mom because I watched her when she recorded her part and I already know what she says. So I watch my mom a couple of times.

Then I see a file that says JTTEST. I look at it for a minute. At first I think I should definitely ask before I open it. But Dad always says that sometimes if you think hard enough, you can come up with more than one way to solve a problem. So I keep thinking, because I would really like to look at that file. And then it works, just like Dad said! I realize that if it's okay that I looked at Mom's part without asking permission, then it's probably okay that I look at a file called JTTEST. And besides, it's only a test, not the real thing.

So I open the file, and JT's face comes up on the computer screen. He says, "Testing one-two-three. Hmmm. Why do people say that, anyway? Testing one-two-three. There must be something more interesting than that to say when you test stuff. Uh, it was nice out today. Probably about seventy-one or seventy-two degrees. School will be out soon, which is good because I'm sick of it. Mom is still pregnant, and, uh, Mary Margaret is still Mary Margaret, of course. Mom says she wants to talk to me about something in private, which is her way of saying she doesn't want Mary Margaret to hear whatever Mom has to say. Not sure what that's all about. Maybe I should practice what I'm going to say for this video now. Ummmm, okay, my name is John Thomas, which is what I used to go by. But when Mary

Margaret was two, she couldn't say John Thomas. The best she could do was to call me Pom-Poms, and that's when I decided I'd rather go by JT. I've been making her pay for that Pom-Poms stuff ever since. You know by now that she's my sister. She's driving all of us crazy with wanting a pet, by the way. But, unlike everything else in our life, this video is supposed to be mostly about me and not about her. Compared to the rest of the people in my family, I'm kind of quiet. I like computers and computer games. I have a Web site, jtcity.com, which would be very cool if only people knew about it, because if they knew about it then they would come and help me build the city. Uh . . . what else? I think of myself as pretty normal, but I look around sometimes and kids I've known since we were in kindergarten are all different from me now. Into sports and stuff that doesn't really fit me." He licks his hand and pats his hair down over his forehead. Then he leans way back in his chair. "Like Duff, who is acting all weird. I mean *Darryl's* acting all weird. I'm not supposed to call him Duff anymore. He's been Duff ever since we became friends, which was like ten years ago. But maybe he's looking for a new name to go with his new personality. And his new friends. He grows a few inches and it's like he grew right out of his brain. Jonah told me it was Duff and his new basketball buddies that trashed Elise's house by putting toilet paper all over the bushes and trees and putting syrup on the screens. I guess Mike and Kevin were laughing so hard that they almost got caught. Oops. I'll have to edit that part out later." JT fiddles with the keyboard and then the movie stops.

Now I get it. JT would like to edit Duff. And he will probably want to edit me, too, if he ever finds out I've been snooping on his computer. Which I will not do again. Ever. I don't need to know what my mom does not want me to know. It would be nice to know, but I don't really need to know, so I am ninety-nine percent sure I will not snoop again.

I wonder what it could be.

7. Starter Pets

If I had to think about what it could be all the time it would make me crazy, so it's a good thing that I am still thinking about getting a pet. Specifically, a pet that my mother would not have to do anything for, which must be what JT meant when he said I should help her out.

The next week we have half days because it's the last week of school before summer vacation, so I have lots of time to think. I hang around on the front porch, watching the pet parade go past our house. It's not a real parade. It's just people taking their dogs to the big park at the end of our street. Lots of them are kind of old people who live in the apartments a few blocks away. I bet since they have pets they don't even mind being wrinkly and gray.

They walk by with their dogs and . . . those plastic bags that they put the doggy-doo in. I don't mind doggy-doo, but ewwwwww! Those plastic bags are just plain ugly, and they don't go with jeans or skirts or anything. They don't even match the dog. Somebody should do something about them.

A boxer walks by with some guy who has even less hair

than my dad. Then Mrs. Fufetti walks by with her miniature poodle, Ceci. "Hi, Mrs. Fufetti," I call. I know her because one time I told her I liked her pink fur coat and then she introduced herself and her dog.

"Hello, dear!" she says. She waves her plastic bag in the air at me as she comes up the walk. "I'm just back from Branson, Missouri, where I heard the most wonderful music!"

I hop down the porch steps so I can pat Ceci's soft curls. "Did Ceci go, too?" I ask.

"Oh, no, dear! She doesn't like anything but classical music. I'm sure country music would give her an eye-twitch. No, I left her at the kennel. They take good care of her there."

"She looks nice," I say.

"So do you, dear. I just love your style. The yellow flowers on that Hawaiian shirt with the blue in your plaid shorts, well, it's nothing less than stunning."

"Thanks, Mrs. Fufetti."

"I hear you're having a baby."

"Not me. My mom's having the baby."

"I meant you're having a baby at your house, dear. Adding a new member to your family."

"Oh."

"It's so exciting! Your mother will be very, very busy! You'll help her, won't you, dear? With the extra chores?"

Wait a minute! No one has said anything to me about extra chores. I already clean my room—once in a blue moon, my mom says, but still!—and clear the table. I also sometimes dust and wash the mirrors. But I like to wash the mirrors, so maybe that doesn't really count as a chore. Either way, I do a lot of chores already.

Ceci pulls hard at her leash. "Oo! Ceci's telling me that I must be off!" Mrs. Fufetti says. "Have a good day, Mary Margaret."

I give Ceci a final scratch behind the ears and then go back up on the porch. I give a big sigh as I watch them walk away because, to tell the truth, I was born to have a pet. I can be patient like Mom wants me to be, but honestly? I'm much better at *doing* than waiting.

There must be something I can do
to get a chipmunk or kangaroo.
There must be something I can do . . . do . . . do.

But before I can finish the rhyme the mailman comes with a special delivery for my mom. She's all excited to get the box and asks me to help her open it. When I do, she says, "Ta-dah!" like whatever is in the box is a big deal. It's an ant farm. My mom laughs and gives me a big hug. "They're for you, Loverly! Now you have lots of pets!"

"Thanks, Mom," I say, even though I'm not sure that ants really count as pets. I mean, I could have gotten them myself off the sidewalk. But Mom is so happy about giving me the ants and I don't want to ruin her good mood, so I put the ant farm on a table in the corner where it won't get bumped. Then I name the ants Brianna, Emma, Sarah, Jessica, Monica, Anna, Julia, and Frank. I can't keep them straight, but they don't seem to care. I feed them a few crumbs and watch them for a little while, but, to tell the truth, watching them makes me dizzy. They run all over the crumbs and each other like wild and crazy ants. JT calls them hyper ants.

When Mom has stopped watching me watch the ants, I go back outside to watch more real pets go by. Pretty soon JT comes out, too. Like I said, Duff isn't around much, and that has been working out pretty good for me because I get to be with JT more. He offers me some of his root beer. I gulp it down. "Whoa!" he says.

I hand it back to him. "Thanks." Then I burp. That makes JT laugh.

"That is rude!" he says.

I say,

"Excuse me, excuse me for being so rude.
It was not my stomach, it was my food.
It got so lonely down there below,
It just popped up to say hello!"

That's just a thing me and JT do after one of us burps. JT taught it to me as soon as I could talk, but back then I said "scoozy, scoozy" because I couldn't talk that good.

"Well? What do you think of the ants?" he asks.

"They're all right," I say. "Just not much fun."

"Maybe they are starter pets, so Mom can find out how good you are at taking care of pets."

That cheers me up a little. I hadn't thought of that. "Maybe," I say.

"Watching the pet parade?" he asks.

"Yeah," I say. "I'm trying to figure out why everyone in the universe gets to have a dog but me. Even people who don't know anything about what goes with what."

"What do you mean?"

Fashion is the one thing I'm smarter about than JT. He doesn't have any fashion sense *at all*. But I try to help him out by explaining, even though he never seems to get it. "They all carry those ugly plastic bags for doggy-doo. If I had a dog, you can bet I'd come up with something better than that. Something that had some style."

"Like what?" he asks.

"I don't know. Leopard print or leather or velvet. Anything would be better than a see-through plastic bag."

"I don't think they could afford to buy a leopard print bag for every time their dog had *to go*," says JT. "That would be like three bags a day or something. That's why people like those plastic bags. They don't cost anything, so people don't feel bad about just throwing them away."

"Well, they should think of something," I say. "Hey, can I have another sip of your root beer?"

"It's all gone."

"I'm going in to get some," I say, standing up. But just then I hear the *slap-slap-slap* of a basketball being dribbled on sidewalk and see three guys coming toward our house. "Hey, isn't that Duff? Who's he with?"

JT looks up and snorts. "The *dudes*. Kevin and Mike. I think playing ball stunts their vocabulary because they go around school saying, '*Dood*.'"

When they get in front of our house, Duff says to the guys, "I'll catch up," and he cuts across our lawn to the front porch.

"Dude!" he says to JT.

JT shoots me a look that means "See what I mean?" And then he says to Duff, "Hey, Duf—I mean Darryl. Did you send in your registration for camp? This year we get to do the three-day survival hike. I already have a new—"

"JT, I decided not to go this year," Duff says.

"But last week you said—"

"I changed my mind," Duff says.

"Oh, so . . ." I can tell JT is trying to think of something to say. "You're still afraid of the dark, huh? Remember that time when you brought a night-light with you? You thought you'd be able to run an extension cord to the tent. Remember that?"

"No, not really," says Duff. "Look, it was fun and everything. I just decided I want to go to basketball camp instead."

"With Mike and Kevin," says JT, slumping his shoulders.

"Well, yeah, they're going, too," Duff says, watching his new friends dribble down the sidewalk.

Then it seems like Duff and JT suddenly remember I'm

right there and JT says to me, "Weren't you going to go get a root beer?"

I know he's just trying to get rid of me, but I am still thirsty, so I go into the house. My mom is sitting at the counter in the kitchen, looking at catalogs.

"How are your ants? Still making themselves at home?"

"Yeah, I think they'd like it here if they'd just relax," I say. "What are you looking at?"

"Oh, I'm just looking at baby stuff. You should see all the different kinds of bottles they have," she says.

Baby stuff. My mom can get pretty carried away with baby talk, so I've learned to get out of there as soon as it sounds like she is going to start up. I grab a root beer out of the refrigerator and take a step toward the door.

"Things sure have changed since you were a baby," she says.

I decide to stay a while longer. If she talks about when I was a baby, then baby talk isn't so bad. "They have?" I ask.

"When you were a baby, they only made glass bottles or plastic ones. The plastic ones did come in different colors, though. You especially liked green ones." She reaches up to scratch my back, which I love. "Later, when you could talk, you'd say, 'G'een, Mama, me wanna g'een one.' You were so cute. But now there are so many bottle options. Look. There are plastic bottles, angled bottles, and bottles with disposable liners."

"What's a disposable liner?" I ask.

"Oh, with those you never have to wash the bottle. See?" She crooks her arm around me so she can point at the picture in the catalog. "The milk actually goes into this liner and not into the bottle itself. Then, when the baby finishes the milk, you just throw the liner away. Nifty, huh?"

I don't say anything. An idea is coming into my head and I need to listen to it. I can tell by how long it's taking that it's going to be a big one.

"Mary Margaret?"

But by then I already have a pencil and some paper and I am hightailing it out the door. I know who is going to do something about those doggy-doo bags. Me. And I know just what I'm going to do.

8. The Poop Pack Plan

I skip out onto the porch, bursting to tell JT my idea. When he and Duff see me, they stop talking, which is great for me because it means I don't have to interrupt.

"JT, listen to this. I have the most fantastic idea about how to—"

"Not now," he says.

"No, wait. I'm not kidding! I'm going to—"

"I'm not kidding, either. Just G.A., okay? Find someone else to tell your great idea to."

"Fine!" What I want to know is why does he have to be so mean about it? Why does everyone have to be so mean about everything? I cannot wait to turn nine because being eight lately has not been great.

I scooter around the block to Andy's house, where I find him in the backyard, practicing—of course. From his crate, Itzy yaps hello, but Andy doesn't even notice me until I get off the scooter and let it fall with a clatter onto the brick path.

"Andy! Listen to this."

"I can't. I have to practice for my audition."

"This will just take a second. I'm going to get a dog!"

"My idea about putting this on your mom's mind worked?"

"Well, no," I say. "That flopped, but I think it was because I did that plan wrong. But I've got an even better idea and I'll do this one right." And then I draw a few pictures and explain everything to Andy. My idea is to make a fabric bag that goes over the plastic bags. "See? People can use the bag I make over and over again. I can help people be more stylish! I will sell the bags and use the money to buy a dog."

"You can't get a dog. Your dad is highly allergic, remember?"

"The dog can live at the kennel! Just like Ceci does when Mrs. Fufetti goes away. I'll earn enough money for a dog and enough to keep it in the kennel!" I do a little tap dance of happiness and a joy-spin around the yard. I am finally going to get a pet, and it's going to be the best pet of all—a D-O-G dog.

"Help me, okay, Andy? Come over right now, okay?"

He plays a quick scale on his violin, then shakes his head. "I told you. I have to practice. My audition for the city youth symphony is tonight."

"It won't take us long, I promise. Please, Andy? You already have a dog, so you don't know what it's like to want one so bad."

Andy looks over at Itzy, who is wagging his whole body

every time we look at him, and sighs. "Yes, I do," he says. "All right."

Back at my house, it takes a while to find the sewing basket and some big enough scraps of material. Then Andy and I try to sew them by hand because Mom won't let me use the sewing machine. But the two we make turn out all bunched up and there's no way to close them. The poop packs we make don't look anything like the ones I saw in my head when I came up with this idea and it makes me mad.

"You're doing it all wrong!" I say to Andy.

"I'm doing what you told me to!"

"No, I *said* to use looser stitches. You're ruining it."

Andy throws the pack he's been working on into my lap. "If you're so good at it, do it yourself! I was just trying to help you, Mary Margaret, because that's what you wanted. And now look," he says, pointing to my clock. "It's five-thirty. My audition is in an hour, and I haven't done my final practice session."

"Audition, schmaudition," I say, flicking the deformed pack out of my lap like it has cooties. "Big deal."

"Maybe not to you, but to me it's a . . . it's a *big dog*."

"Don't you mean big deal?" I ask.

"No, I mean big dog," he says, getting up to leave. "Because pet talk is the only talk you understand."

He's wrong. I don't get *any* of his talk. Or maybe I just don't want to.

But I don't need Andy. JT will understand. *He'll* help me

and *he'll* be able to make the poop packs turn out right. But when I get to his bedroom door, I hear my dad and him talking. I stand very still and quiet so that I can listen.

". . . sorry he's not going," my dad is saying. "You'll make other friends at camp, though. Just go right up, introduce yourself, and then ask the person about himself. People can't resist talking about themselves."

"It's not that," says JT.

"It's not?"

"Maybe it's part of it. I don't know. Everything is . . . weird right now. People are weird and . . . different."

"People change, JT. Even adults change sometimes."

I picture my mom, who is growing bigger by the minute, and think, You can say that again.

JT says, "Well, I wish they would change back."

"Sometimes they do; sometimes they don't," my dad says. "Sometimes they try on new attitudes or personalities, just like you try on a new pair of tennis shoes to see if they fit. And if they like the new personality, they stay that way."

JT mumbles something I can't hear.

After a minute Dad says, "Hey, I have an idea. Let's go out to Mad Dogs and get a couple of those hot dogs you like so much—just you and me. Just the guys."

I barely have time to skedaddle back to my room without getting caught. Dad knocks on my door and tells me where they are going. Then he says, "Mom's resting, so don't bother her. I'll bring you back a Devil Dog." I pretend

I didn't already know that they are going, but I don't fuss about not going along.

I go back to working on poop packs. I know the way they should look, but no matter how hard I try, I can't make them look that way. And every pack is turning out to be a different size, even though I'm trying to make them all the same. And, worst of all, I keep sticking myself with the needle. By the time they get back with my Devil Dog, I'm in a worse mood than ever.

JT, though, seems to be in a better mood. After I eat, I show him what I'm doing. He picks up the poop packs and looks at the Band-Aids on my finger. Then he says, "Mary-Maker, what you need is the sewing machine."

There's a problem with that idea, though. My mother won't let me use the sewing machine by myself. And I don't want to ask her to help me because she has a lot on her mind—and one of those things is a pet for me. If helping me with poop packs is also on her mind, then she might stop thinking about getting me something other than ants as a pet. My mom used to be able to keep a lot more things on her mind at one time, but the baby-that-is-not-even-here-yet changed all that. What I need is someone else to help me. What I need is JT.

"JT, will you help me?"

"Ohhhhh, no," he says. "No way, no how. Forget it!"

"JT, please?"

"No. Look, it's not going to work, anyway. Your idea is good, but you'll never save that kind of money."

"I will too!" I say. "Just you wait and see."

"I'll wait and see, but I won't sew. Not on your life. If the guys in my class found out—or even if the girls found out . . . Look, Mary Margaret. I'm not like other kids my age."

JT is kind of short and skinny, has braces, and wears tennis shoes with everything. He's *exactly* like other kids his age. "Sure you are!" I say.

"No, I'm not. Kids my age hang out in groups. But me? I mostly just hang out with me."

"Oh, yeah, because Duff has new friends."

JT squinches his eyes up and looks at me. "How did you know Duff has new friends?"

Uh-oh. I start with my nervous habit of talking real fast. "Well, uh, I guess I just thought since he wasn't hanging around here anymore that he must be hanging out, ummm, somewhere with somebody and that those somebodies must be his friends. And we did see him the other day with—what were those guys' names? You know, the dudes?" He is still looking at me, chewing on his thumbnail. I know if he chews on it long enough he will probably figure out that I was on his computer in places where I definitely should not have been. So I say, "What do you mean kids hang out in groups?"

He has to take his thumbnail out of his mouth to answer me, so my plan works. He stops thinking. "Like if you play sports, you hang out with other kids who play sports."

"Well, we do that, too," I say. I know I have to keep the

conversation going. "If you want to play soccer at recess, then you're with everyone else playing soccer."

"It's not really the same. What about if you have indoor recess or after school? Do you hang out with the kids you were playing soccer with? Do you eat lunch with them?"

"No-o-o. Why would I do that? I hang around with Tina and Ally or Bev and Julee or Sammy, sometimes."

"And what about the next day?" JT says. "Is it that same group playing soccer again?"

"It's just whoever wants to play soccer."

"It's not that easy at my age," he says. "If you're into a sport, you not only play the sport with the same people, you also eat lunch with those people. And hang out in the hall with them. And go to the mall with them on the weekends."

"Weird," I say. "Why?"

"It's just the way it is. Kids my age think it's weird if you *don't* hang out in a crowd. So I'm already different that way. And if word ever got out that I was sewing? Bad news."

"But they wouldn't have to know," I say. "I am very good at keeping secrets. I kept the secret about Mom being pregnant. I only told one person."

"Yeah—Jolene! And she told everyone else in the neighborhood."

"But I learned. I'll be better with this secret."

JT shakes his head. "Negatory. That's all. Just no. Why can't you be happy with your ant farm?"

"They aren't real pets, JT, and you know it."

"Yeah, ants are a sorry excuse for a pet," he says. "It's pretty pathetic, when you think about it."

"Yeah. So is my life. Pathetic."

He laughs at that. "Aren't you exaggerating a little, Melodra-Margaret?"

I don't think I'm exaggerating. I *never ever* get what I want. And I'm sick of JT making jokes with my name.

"Quit it, JT! I can't have the thing I want more than anything because it makes Dad sneeze. Mom says to be patient, which I was, and then gets me *ants* as *pets*. And then I get all excited about making these dumb packs so I can get a dog. But I can't use the sewing machine alone, and you won't help. So I can't even do that. Just G.A."

When he doesn't G.A., I do. At least I try to, but then JT says, "Where do you think you're going?"

"I *think* I'm going to get my kiki," I say, in a way that means "Don't try to stop me."

He grabs the back of my Lycra shirt so that it stretches way out until finally I have to stop. "Your *kiki?* Hasn't that thing decomposed by now? And stuff like that is for *little* kids!"

"Let go, JT!" I twist away so he has to let go of my shirt. "What's the big deal about being big anyway?"

"You get to do more stuff, I guess."

"No, *you* get to do more stuff! I don't. Except chores. I'll have to do more chores. Mrs. Fufetti says so."

He steps between me and the door. "You're right," he says.

It always confuses me when he says, "You're right" when we're in the middle of a fight. I think it should be against the rules. I mean, in order to fight, the people fighting have to be on different sides, and if someone says "You're right," then you're both on the same side. Which is why it's confusing.

I finally say, "I am? I really will have to do more chores?"

"No. Well, yes, actually. What I mean is things are bad for you right now, and it's only going to get worse."

"It is?"

"Wait until the baby comes. I remember when you were born. Mom and Dad were so busy taking care of you, they forgot to feed me."

"They did not!"

"Seriously. Sit down, and I'll tell you about it."

So I sit back down on the steps and JT sits down next to me.

"Yeah," he says, "they were pretty much useless for three months. You were a screamer, so they got no sleep."

"I was not! Mom just told me I was cute as a baby."

"That came later. Much later."

"What did you do when they forgot to feed you?"

"I finished off a box of cookies. I knew I should have eaten something healthy, but I was too short to reach the ice cream. Then I did the laundry, raked the yard, took out the trash, washed the dishes, and shopped for groceries. *And* I made dinner for eighteen people on Thanksgiving."

I believe him for about half a minute. He has a way of

saying stuff that makes you believe him, even when he's kidding. He learned that from Dad. "You did not!" I say.

He shrugs. "All I'm saying is, things might get worse before they get better."

Like I said, JT jokes around a lot, so I don't believe him about that. Not much, anyway.

"I would just like to see my kiki," I say, mostly to myself.

JT doesn't say anything for a minute, but then he throws his arm over my shoulders. "You know, I've been thinking, and you're right about those bags that people with dogs carry. Someone has got to do something about them."

"You mean . . . ?"

"Yes. I'll help you make some poop packs."

"Thanks, JT! You're the best!"

"Yeah, well, maybe. But listen. If you tell anyone outside of this family that I'm sewing, there will be serious consequences."

"Like . . ."

"Like I'll put an embarrassing story about you on my Web site."

I won't tell anyone. And even if I did, I wouldn't be worried about JT saying something about me on his site. No one ever goes there, anyway.

Before bed I tell my parents that I am going to get a dog and keep it at a kennel. Then I tell them how I am going to earn the money all by myself.

"*All* by yourself?" JT says.

"Well, all by myself but with JT's help," I say. "He's going to sew the poop packs. What do you think?"

My dad taps his top lip fast. "Hmm. It would take a while. Quite a while. But good for you! There's the old Anderson pluck."

"What's pluck?"

"Trying to get what you want, even when things look bad. Taking things into your own hands. Taking action on a problem. That sort of thing."

"What Dad means is that there's something you want, and you have a plan to get it," says my mom. "Making those packs is a smart idea," she says. "But can't you call them something else?"

"It is descriptive, though," says my dad. "You do want buyers to know exactly what it is."

My mom frowns at my dad. "It's *too* descriptive. How about something a little daintier?"

"Daintier, huh?" says JT. "Okay, poop purses. Purses are daintier than packs."

My mom rolls her eyes. "Purse is fine. The other word has got to go. How about doggy-doo purses?"

"It doesn't exactly roll off the tongue," my dad says. "What are some other words for purse or pack? Case, carrier, backpack . . ."

"Bag or tote," my mom adds. "Or—"

I clap my hands over my ears because another idea is coming into my head and I can't hear it with them talking. "Tote!" I shout. "We'll call them Number Two Totes!"

"That's it!" Dad and JT say at the same time.

My mom says, "I guess it is slightly more civilized than poop pack."

I spend the first few days of summer vacation getting ready to make Number Two Totes. My mom is going to the fabric store and she offers to take me along. On the way to the store, I lay out my money in my lap and count it. With the $10.00 I got from Rat Man and some saved allowance money, I have $17.32.

"Where did you get all that money?" my mom asks.

"Well, ahhh, someone paid me to help them find something of theirs a while ago," I say. Then I fiddle with the CD player, which I know she hates, so that the next thing she will say to me is "Stop fiddling with the stereo!" instead of "What did you help them find?"

At the store, I look at different fabrics for a while. Then I buy leopard skin print, red velvet, pink fur fabric that's exactly like the fur of Mrs. Fufetti's coat, and—best of all—tie-dye spandex with sparkles. I wonder if maybe Andy would like a tie made out of the spandex but decide I just need to learn how to do the totes first. Ties will have to come later.

When we get home, Mom helps me cut a cardboard rectangle. Then all I have to do is set the piece of cardboard on the material, trace around it, and cut the rectangle out. Already I can tell that these are going to be better than the other ones Andy and I tried to make. Still, some of the pieces I cut are kind of funny looking because I'm not that good at cutting straight yet.

"No one will notice on a galloping pony," my mom says.

"Mom, these are for *dogs*," I say.

"Well, no one will notice on a galloping dog, either," she says, laying some more fabric out. "It's nice being together like this, isn't it, Loverly? So quiet and peaceful." She stops cutting and scratches her tummy. "I guess we should enjoy the quiet while it lasts."

"Yeah, I guess," I say. She must be thinking about what she has to do next—maybe something like vacuuming, which is very loud.

"Before long, I won't have time to do anything like this," she says.

I know she means she won't have time for sewing. I wonder what else she won't have time for.

9. Syrup Head

JT isn't very excited about helping me sew the Number Two Totes, but finally he makes one, and I finish it by threading cord around the top so there's a way to close it. He says there definitely needs to be a way to close the tote because once you put number two in there, you don't want to be able to see or smell it.

I don't mean to brag or anything, but it looks pretty good when we're done. It's the right shape and it's flat and the cord works great. I beg JT to make more, but he just says, "I have my limits."

After a few days of him saying that, I know what "I have my limits" means. It means that he'll only work on them when he doesn't have anything better to do. I guess when you're JT, there's *always* something better to do, even when Duff isn't around. Because JT loves the computer and jtcity.com, and the computer and jtcity.com are always there, on the old table in the living room, waiting for him.

All I really want to do is work on the totes, so there is never something better for me to do, which means I have to find some things to do so I don't die of boredom. During the first weeks of summer I paint and draw a lot of pictures; write notes to my grandpa and grandma; and teach myself to do a flip on the monkey bars, scooter backward (harder than it looks!), make scrambled eggs in the microwave, and a bunch of other stuff.

Sometimes I go over to Andy's house to play with Itzy, but Andy doesn't play with us much. He'll be out in the backyard with us, but all he does is practice his violin. Even though I get to play with Itzy, which is what I thought I wanted to do, something doesn't feel right. It feels like I'm drinking pop that's lost its fizz—it's still sweet but not all that interesting.

On the day JT finishes the fifth tote, I think I finally have enough to set up my stand on the sidewalk. I call up Andy and ask him if he'll come help me sell them.

"I don't think so," he says. "I probably *wouldn't do it right*. I'd probably *ruin* it."

"I didn't really mean all that," I say. "I was frustrated."

"It was still rude," he says. "And you never even asked if I got into the symphony."

"Did you?"

"No."

"Because of me?"

"Right, all because of you and those stupid poop packs," he says. But then he's quiet for a minute. "No, not *all* because of you. I shouldn't have waited until right before auditions to practice."

"Do you have to practice now?"

"I should," he says. "But . . . I could do it there on your sidewalk instead of in my backyard, I guess. If you want me to."

That makes me smile. "Yeah! That will attract a lot of business!"

By the time I get the table set up outside and bring all the totes out and arrange them on the table, Andy has come over. All we need to do is to wait for the pet parade to begin. It's a nice day, and the windows in our house are open, so we can hear the *click-click-click*ing sound that JT's keyboard makes when he types. We can even hear him complain, "Oh, man!" when something goes wrong for him.

But pretty soon we have more interesting things to do. First comes Mr. Man-in-Suit with his Jack Russell terrier.

I smile big. "Hello!"

"Hello. Nice music there."

"Yeah, Andy is a good violinist. Would you like to buy a Number Two Tote?"

"A what?"

"A Number Two Tote."

"I don't know. What's it for?"

I lean in close to the man. "Doggy-doo," I whisper.

"Is that right?" he says, raising his eyebrows.

"Yes," I say. "You still put . . . *it* in that plastic bag you've got there, but then you drop the plastic bag into the tote so no one has to look at *it*. Like my mom always says, 'Out of sight, out of mind.'"

"Let me give it some thought," he says.

Then comes a yellow Lab and Mrs. Mother-in-Shorts, walking fast, pushing a stroller that has a kid and a baby in it.

"Hello!" I say. "Would you like to buy a—"

"On a—*huff huff*—power walk—*huff huff*—keep heart rate up."

"Oh, okay!" I call after her. I give a little wave. "Yeah . . . okay."

The yellow Lab turns his head to look back at me. Either he's interested in the totes or he's hoping I'll rescue him; I can't tell which. Andy thinks the dog looked back because he liked the music he was playing.

Nobody else is coming down the sidewalk, so Andy and I talk for a while about what kind of dog I should buy. Then Mr. Jacobs comes with his beagle, Happy.

"Hello, Mr. Jacobs." He's an oldish man who lives a couple of houses down from us. He always lets me pet Happy.

"Hello, there, Mary Margaret. How are you today?"

"Fine. I'm selling Number Two Totes." And I explain the idea to him while I scratch Happy's ears.

"Why, I think that's quite creative!" he says. "Let me take a look." He picks up the pink fur one. "My. That's quite . . . furry, isn't it?" he says. While he's looking at the others he says, "Say, I understand your mom's going to have a baby. What do you think about that?"

"Oh, we're excited," I say. "Mostly."

He puts down the leopard-print tote. "I'm sorry, Mary Margaret. I just don't see anything here that's my style."

I kind of see what he means.

"Good luck, though," he says.

I am starting to wonder if this will be a no-thank-you day when Mrs. Fufetti and Ceci walk by.

"I haven't seen you in a long time, Mary Margaret. I've been in Pennsylvania visiting my grandchildren," she says. "How is your summer going?"

"Pretty good," I say. "This is my friend Andy. He plays the violin."

"He plays it very well," she says.

"He's keeping me company while I sell my Number Two Totes." Then I explain what they are and how they work.

"Oooo!" she says. "That's fabulous! I love that pink fur one. That will match my winter coat perfectly!"

"It's one of a kind," I say. "JT said he wouldn't make another." He said that because, when we were making that one, the fur gummed up the sewing machine and we spent a long time pulling little pieces of fur out of the machine. We are not allowed to use swear words in our house, but I'm pretty sure he was thinking some of them when that happened.

"He won't, eh?" she says. "In that case, I'd better snap it up! How much are they?"

"Five dollars."

She gives me a five-dollar bill.

"Thank you!" I say. "This is the first one I've sold."

"I think you'll sell lots of others," she says. "I'll tell my friends all about it. They are all such gossips, soon the whole town will know."

After that I'm feeling pretty happy—until Duff and Kevin and Mike walk up. And that's when I understand why they call each other *dude*. Since they all wear the same thing—baggy shorts, torn T-shirts, sunglasses, and baseball caps turned around backward—they probably can't tell who is who. They call each other dude so they don't have to figure it out! Kind of lazy of them, I think.

Anyway, the first thing they do is to start pawing my totes. "What are these things?" Duff asks.

"They look like little *pur*-ses," sings Kevin (I think), dangling one by the cord from his little finger.

Mike (I think) walks over to Andy, who is sitting on the grass, plucking his violin strings like it's a guitar. He looks down on Andy and says, "Hey, do you play with these *pur*-ses? I gotta tell you, Junior, *pur*-ses can turn you into a girl. Real men don't go near purses, right, little guy?" Mike nudges Andy with his toe. "Right?"

Kevin points to the violin. "And they don't play violins, either."

Andy doesn't say anything. He just looks away, then pulls his violin case over to him and carefully puts his violin away. He snaps the case closed and fastens the clasps, then throws his arm over the case, like he's guarding it.

Kevin shrugs and then joins Mike and Duff, who have started tossing the tote around like it's a hot potato, squealing whenever they have to touch it.

"Stop it!" I say. "Give it back!"

Duff catches it and says, "Oooh! Look at me! I've got Minor-Margaret's pur-urse!"

That's it for me. I let JT tease me about my name because it's just what he does. He's not mean about it or anything. But nobody else gets to, especially not someone who is making fun of my Number Two Totes and my friend. Especially not someone who is being a jerk to my brother. Especially not someone who is practically a criminal. Which is what I'm thinking when I shout, "My name is Mary Margaret, *SYRUP HEAD!*"

All of the dudes freeze.

"*What* did you call me?" Duff asks.

"Syrup Head," I say. "Because . . ." I fake a cough to give myself more time to think. "Because you used to be sweet and now you're mean."

The dudes laugh then. "Yeah, you're right about that!" one of them says. Then they all leave.

Andy flops down on the grass beside his violin case and closes his eyes. As I watch the dudes leave, I hear JT slamming the window. It must be getting too hot in there for him, and he's going to turn on the air conditioner. If he thinks it's too hot in there, I think, he should try being out here in the sun.

We stay out for a while longer, hoping for more customers, but pretty soon we start feeling like we are baked potatoes in an oven because that's how hot we are. Andy goes home and I go inside to tell JT that we need to make more totes. He's in his room with the door closed.

I knock. "JT?" But he doesn't answer. I knock harder and then he comes to the door wearing headphones—and a scowl.

"What?"

"Mrs. Fufetti says that pretty soon the whole town will know about the totes because of her gossipy friends. I think we should make some more."

"No." Then he closes the door in my face.

"But you said—"

"I don't care what I said. I changed my mind," he yells through the door. I can tell by his tone of voice that he means it.

"But that's not fair!"

"Yeah? Well whoever said life was fair? Just go back to selling your totes and leave me alone."

"I would—if *your* dumb friends would just leave us alone!"

"Mm-nm-en," he mumbles.

"What?"

"THEY'RE NOT MY FRIENDS!" he yells. "And besides, it's none of your business."

"Oh," I say, because it's pretty hard to blame him for his dumb friends if they aren't his friends.

It's not like JT to change his mind. Usually I can count on him. One thing is for sure. He's right about people being all different and weird lately. But he doesn't know that he's one of them.

Walking by the computer, I remember his JTTEST file.

Maybe he told the computer why he won't help me anymore. If he did, I have a right to know. He's wrong about it not being my business. It is my business—my Number Two Tote business.

This time I see a new file called TOPSECRET. I turn the volume way down and then open the file quickly. "Mom finally snagged me when Mary Magnet wasn't around," JT says. I hold my breath. Will he say what she said? "She told me a top-level secret. She said that once Mary Margaret starts doing more chores and stuff around the house, not just her own stuff but whatever needs to be done, she's going to let her take riding lessons. Mom said something about wanting Mary Margaret to take the initiative. Mom wants me to tell her when I see Mary Margaret doing stuff without being asked. So I said, 'Sure, I'll help out.' I mean, it's not like I have anything more interesting going on at the moment."

I am so surprised that I almost forget to stop holding my breath. And then I breathe out real slow. Riding lessons! It's not the same thing as having my own pet, but WOW! I'll get to be around horses!

I close the file. I should check on my ants sometime, but I decide to wait until someone is around to *see* me check on my ants, because that is the way that I'll get riding lessons. JT is not coming out of his room ever again, or at least that's what it seems like, so I wait until my dad gets home to put a few crumbs and a drop of water into the ant farm.

That's when I see that one of them has died. I think it's Frank.

I'm not that attached to my ants, so I'm not that sad about it. But what if my mom thinks it's my fault that Frank died? I flop facedown on the couch. "This pet thing is just not going that well for me," I say.

Dad sits on the arm of the couch, which my mom never lets *me* do. "I know that's the way it feels right now," he says. "But the instructions said that ants don't live very long. And eventually you'll get another pet. Eventually, after—"

I groan. "I know, I know. After the *baby*. I have to be *patient*."

He tugs on his cap. "Hey, I've got an idea!" he says. "How about you pick the baby's name?"

I raise my head up off the couch cushion. "Me? I get to pick the baby's name?"

"Wait. Mom might want to pick the first name," my dad says. "How about the middle name? You can pick that."

"*Any* middle name I want?"

"Within reason," he says. "No four-letter words. No insults. That kind of thing."

I know he's trying to cheer me up, but naming the baby? Yeah, that sounds like fun. "Okay," I say.

JT and Dad and me let the ants go in the yard. We think they should be free for at least part of life. I make up a good-bye poem:

Brianna, Emma, and Sarah,
You didn't have any hair-ah.
Jessica, Monica, Anna,
You ate a little banana.
Julia, you were so little and sweet,
I wish I could have gotten six little shoes for your
six little feet.
Having you all as pets wasn't that much fu-un,
But I guess it was better than nuth-un.

We watch them run around in little circles. I want to wave good-bye to them, but they never actually leave the patio. They are still racing around and bumping into each other when we give up and leave.

A little while later Mom comes home. She gives me a hug and then sees the empty ant farm. "Hey, what happened to the ants?" she asks.

"One died, and we decided to let the rest go," I say. I put my hand on her belly and pretend there's a baby dolphin flopping around in there, because that's the way it looks sometimes to me. I give her another hug. If I squeeze her, my arms can still fit all the way around her.

My mom looks like she's going to cry.

"Did you cut up some onions at your meeting?" I ask.

She says no, it's the ants. Then she does cry a little.

"It wasn't my fault," I say. "I took very good care of them."

"I know you did," she says. "It's not that."

"Then why are you crying? Do you miss them?" I ask. "We can visit them, if you want. I bet they are all still running in circles on the patio."

She sniffles. "It's silly," she says. "They are just ants."

She and my dad look at each other. "Hormones," they say together.

I know all about those. At the same time my mom got the baby-that-is-not-here-yet she also got the hormones. It's their job to help the baby grow, but sometimes they also make my mom cranky or sad or tired. My dad says that when the baby comes out, the hormones will, too.

My mom keeps one arm around me and slides the other one around my dad's waist. "How are you doing?" she says to me. "Do you feel sad about the ants?"

"I did," I say, "but then Dad cheered me up. He told me I could name the baby."

"He told you that you could name the baby," she says.

"The middle name," says my dad, smiling nervously.

"I think I'm going to pick *Third* for the baby's middle name," I say.

"*Third*," my mom says.

"Because the baby will be the third kid in this family," I say. "What do you think?"

"I'll get back to you on that," my mom says to me. She kicks off her meeting shoes. "I would give my eyeteeth for a cup of coffee. But I guess I'll lie down instead."

I follow her upstairs and climb into bed with her.

That makes her smile. "Hi, snuggle bunny," she says.

"Hi, stummy drummy," I say. That's a thing we do, my mom and me. Make up silly names for each other.

"Stummy drummy? That's a new one!"

"Stomach. Plus tummy. Plus drum."

"Just what I always wanted to be," she says. "A stummy drummy mummy."

She pulls me in close, but that ball of baby is right in my back. So we try lying on our backs. Then on our sides again. "Boy, that baby sure makes it hard to get comfortable," I say.

"Tell me about it," she says.

10. The Baddest Chore of All

JT is pretty much a hermit for the next few days. He says he's busy getting ready for summer camp, but he doesn't even have his suitcase out yet. And when he does come out of his room, he's only out for a few minutes before he disappears again, so I don't have time to even start doing a chore. If things keep going like this, he'll never catch me taking the initiative.

After a few days of me being very frustrated, I come up with a way to solve that problem. I decide to make up a list of chores I can do so whenever he comes out of his room I don't have to quick think up something to do. I can just look at the list and start doing one of the chores that's on it.

I get some grapes for a snack and then start my list. To make it more fun, I come up with a chore every time I eat a grape. When the grapes are gone, my list will be done.

EMPTEE TRASH
PUT AWAY LAWNDRY
EMPTEE DISH WASHER
VACKUME

I still have six grapes left to eat. So I scratch out PUT
AWAY LAWNDRY and write

PUT AWAY MOM'S LAWNDRY
PUT AWAY DAD'S LAWNDRY
PUT AWAY JT'S LAWNDRY (if he lets me in)

Then I scratch out VACKUME and write

VACKUME LIVING ROOM
VACKUME MOM'S BEDROOM
VACKUME JT'S BEDROOM (if he lets me in)

There. Because I don't have any grapes left to eat, I
don't have to add any more chores. Then I draw pictures
next to each thing on my list because I like to draw and I
think lists are more interesting when they have pictures
and not just words.

When I throw the grape stem away, I notice that the
trash does need to be emptied. I could do it, but making that
list was a big job and I need to rest. Also, no one is around
right now to see me be responsible by doing something
without being asked. So I wait until JT comes out of his
room and goes into the kitchen.

I hop right up and follow him. When he unwraps his
granola bar and puts the wrapper on the table, I throw it in
the trash for him. "Looks like the trash is getting full," I say.

I glance over at JT, who is chugging down his milk. "I guess I might as well go ahead and empty it."

JT looks at me kind of funny. "What would make you do a nice thing like that?"

"Someone has to."

"Yeah, usually me."

I shrug and take the trash out to the garage. When I come back, JT is heading toward the living room, pulling the vacuum behind him. "Let me do that," I say.

"I'm supposed to," he says.

"But I noticed that it really needed to be done. I was going to do it," I say, "right after I emptied the trash. I really want to do it."

"Suit yourself," he grumbles. He scowls at me before he disappears again into his room. I don't know why he's not happy about me doing his chores. Sometimes brothers can be so strange.

I never do figure what's going on with JT, because the next day he leaves for camp. I give him a hug good-bye, but he doesn't exactly hug me back, so it feels like I'm hugging a tree instead of JT. At least he's smiling as he and Dad drive away. "Take it easy, Mary Maid," he yells out the window. "KWIM?" And then he's gone.

The next day, Andy tells me he's leaving, too. "What do you mean you're going to music camp?" I ask him while trying to fend off Itzy's licks. "How come you didn't tell me before?"

"I didn't know until today," he says. "I was on a wait list

at this violin camp in New York that's really hard to get into, and they just called to say someone dropped out. So I get to go. Mom's driving me. She's going to spend the week with my aunt who lives near there."

"So it'll just be your dad and Itzy here?"

"Yeah. You can still come and play with Itzy, though."

"What about selling Number Two Totes?" I ask.

"I guess just do it by yourself. You don't need me for that."

I don't want to think about him going away, so I tell him all about how JT said I'll be able to take riding lessons if I do a bunch of chores. Andy says he hopes that I do get riding lessons because he knows how much I want them. Then he doesn't say anything and so it's quiet for a minute, and I'm thinking about what I'll be doing while he's gone and what my life will be like without him or JT around and how boring it will probably be because even my kid-neighbors Jessie and Jolene have gone away for a few weeks. And so I'm wondering why stuff like this always happens to me. Itzy is still bounding around like a rubber ball and I watch him jump up and try to lick Andy's face. That's when I notice that Andy looks different, like maybe he's not feeling so good.

"What's wrong?" I ask. "Did you eat a bad hot dog or something?"

"No. It's just that I've never been to an overnight camp before. I want to go. But I *don't* want to go. KWIM?"

He got that KWIM stuff from me, of course. But suddenly I think I do know what he means. "You mean you're kind of excited but kind of scared, too?" I say. "Like when you go on a roller coaster because you want to, but then as the roller coaster is climbing up that first hill, you're wondering if it's the dumbest thing you've ever done?"

"Yes, and . . ."

"And you're worried that it will be hard to make friends? And you don't know where you'll be sleeping—top bunk or bottom? And if it's on the top, will you fall when you're trying to climb down to go to the bathroom in the middle of the night? And how far away will the bathroom be, anyway?"

"Yeah, and—"

But now that I've put myself in Andy's shoes, it seems like I'm in his head, too, thinking everything that he's thinking. "And what if the only food they serve is food you hate like liver and peas? And what if you're the worst player there? What if there's a bully and he decides to pick on nobody but you? What if, in the middle of the night, he decides to put your hand in a bowl of warm water so you'll pee in your bed?" Then I gasp because I have just thought of the worst thing of all. *"What if nobody likes you and you have to eat every single meal sitting by yourself? Is that what you mean?"* I ask.

When Andy looks at me, his eyes are wide. "Yeah. And some of that stuff I hadn't even thought of yet."

We stare at each other for a few minutes, letting the worry sink in. No wonder Andy feels sick. I'd like to be able to help him, but what can I do? I can't go with him. I don't even have any ideas on what to do about all that stuff. But then I remember what I heard my dad telling JT when he found out Duff wasn't going to camp.

So I say to Andy, "All you have to do is introduce yourself and then ask the other person about himself. My dad says people love to talk about themselves. Then, once you've made a friend, you won't be alone. You'll still have to figure out that other stuff about bunks and bathrooms and bullies, but you'll do it together."

"Maybe," says Andy.

"Let's practice," I say. We both stand up. "First introduce yourself; then ask about me."

Andy looks at the ground. "My name is Andy," he says.

"That was okay," I say, "but look at me when you say it. And be friendlier."

He tries it again. "Hi. My name is Andy," he says, looking right at me. "What's yours?"

"Mary Margaret," I say. "Nice to meet you." Then I whisper, "Now ask me about myself."

"Ask you what?"

"Anything! Where I live, what instrument do I play, have I been to this camp before."

By the time we're done practicing, Andy seems a little happier. "So all I have to do is ask them about themselves, huh?"

"That's what my dad says," I say. "And I'd say he's right about seventy-five percent of the time."

"Thanks, Mary Margaret, and I hope you get those riding lessons."

I do, too. Which is why I start doing chores. A *lot* of chores. I sweep. I dust. I clean mirrors and sinks and counters. I vacuum rooms and hallways and the cracks of the couch, where I find cracker crumbs, two pennies, and my dinosaur Gary's collar. I set the table, clear the table, and put the plates and silverware in the dishwasher. I carry dirty clothes to the washer and fold and put away clean clothes.

At first my mom is surprised. "Have you seen my daughter?" she says to me. "Her name is Mary Margaret, and she looks a lot like you, but you're a lot better at helping out."

She's joking, of course. "Mo-om," I say. "You know it's me." Still, I can't help smiling.

"Thank you, Loverly, for helping me." She gives me a big hug. The baby kicks me right in the cheek, but the hug still feels good. I feel good.

She does not say anything about riding lessons, even after I've been doing chores for days and days. I can't understand it. Maybe there's something I'm not doing right. That's when I decide that my mom must be waiting for me to do more than just an ordinary chore. To earn those riding lessons, I need to do an extraordinary chore. The baddest chore of all. A chore that will show my mom for real and for true that I can handle anything.

In other words, I'll have to clean the toilet.

I go to the cupboard where Mom keeps the cleaning supplies. There are spray bottles and cans and boxes. Lots of them. I'm not sure which to use. All of them have exclamation marks, so they all must be very important. One says "New Mountain Spring Scent!" I think Mom would like the toilet to smell like a new mountain spring, so I dump some of that in. Another says "Bleaches out tough stains so surfaces sparkle like new!" Our toilet is old and it has a few stains and I think Mom would be happy if it sparkled like new. When I put that in the toilet, too, the water starts to bubble.

It also smells strong. Clean, I guess, but very strong. So I put some cleaner from the box that says "Eliminates Unwanted Odor!" because I sure would like to eliminate this strong odor. That just makes it smell worse. But I've come in to do the job that will get me the riding lessons and I'm going to do that job no matter what. I pick up the toilet brush, bend over, and take a few deep breaths. . . .

I can't say what happens next because all of a sudden I am on the floor and my mom is dragging me out of the bathroom into the hall, yelling "Mary Margaret! Mary Margaret!"

"What? What?" I say.

"What on earth were you trying to do?"

"What happened?" I ask. "Everything looks soft and spongy."

"You fainted," she says, "probably from all the chemical fumes in those products."

"Oh."

"What were you trying to do?"

"Clean the toilet," I say. I feel kind of woozy.

"Why?"

"Because I want riding lessons," I say.

"Riding lessons! What does cleaning toilets have to do with riding lessons?" She sounds very surprised, like she has never heard of this idea before.

When I don't feel so good, which I don't at the moment, I don't think so good. This must be why everything burbles right out of my mouth, like water burbles out of a hose. "JT said that you said if I started doing more chores and showed I was responsible, then I would get to take riding lessons," I say. "So I was doing lots of chores, but you still weren't saying anything about riding lessons so I wanted to do the biggest, baddest chore of all."

My mom frowns and then sits down. "Listen, honey. I never said anything like that to JT. When did he tell you that?"

I try to swallow, but nothing goes down my throat. "He didn't *exactly* say it to me. He said it to the camera on his computer."

"And you overheard him saying it?"

I would like to lie. I really, really would like to lie right now, but I don't. "No. I opened his file and watched him say it."

"So you were snooping around where you didn't have permission to be. How many times did you snoop, Mary Margaret?"

"A few," I say.

My mom shakes her head back and forth, back and forth, very slowly, which means she is disappointed in me. I wish she was mad instead. "I think I see what went on here," she says. "JT realized what you were doing. He was angry about it—you know how he feels about his things—"

"No admission without permission," I say quietly.

"Right—no admission without permission—and so he

tricked you. He lied on the tape to get back at you for snooping. It was wrong of him to bait you, but you shouldn't have been snooping."

Then she sends me to my room to think things over.

I write Andy a postcard and tell him exactly what I think.

Dear Andy,
My life stinks. I did the chores, but I won't get any riding
lessons because all that was a big, fat LIE that JT told to
his computer. He knew I would snoop and he wanted me to
quit it so he dreamed up this stupid trick. I wish I didn't
have a know-it-all brother. If I'm not here when you get
back, I ran away. Have a good life.

And then I sign my name. If my mother ever lets me out of my room, I'll mail it. I won't run away, though, because I think it takes at least forty dollars to be able to run away, and I don't have that much.

I lie down on my bed and stare at the ceiling. At least now I know why JT was acting weird before he left for camp. I don't really wish I didn't have JT. What I really wish is that JT wouldn't be mad at me, even though none of that stuff was my fault. If he hadn't . . . if he hadn't . . . But I can't think of an end to that sentence and so maybe some of it was my fault. What I really wish is that my mom and me would be like peanut butter and jelly again—stuck together. What I really wish is that all of us would just go back to normal.

Later JT calls from camp and Mom talks to him for a

while and even though I can't hear what she's saying, her voice is quiet and serious so I know she's disappointed in him, too. When she's done talking to him, she tries to hand me the phone. I shake my head.

"Take it," she whispers.

"I don't want to."

"I know you don't want to, but do it anyway. *Apologize*," she says firmly.

I roll my eyes but take the phone because I don't have a choice.

"I'm sorry I snooped, JT," I say.

"You should be," he says.

"I just wanted to find out why you were acting weird," I say. "Why you suddenly wouldn't help me after you told me that you would."

"It's not any of your business," he says.

"You didn't have to be so mean about it."

"Look. Nobody likes to be laughed at, okay?"

"What do you mean? I never did that."

"No, *you* didn't."

If I didn't, who did? And then I remember the day when Duff and the dudes made fun of our totes and I remember that I could hear JT typing on his computer. And if I could hear what JT was doing inside the house, then he could hear what Duff was saying outside the house.

"Oh, you heard Duff—"

"Look. I just changed my mind," he says. "It's a free country."

"Unless you're a slave," I say. "Doing all kinds of work for free."

"Yeah, that was pretty mean," he says, doing that thing again where he agrees with me right in the middle of a fight. "At first I thought you deserved it, but I started to feel guilty after a few days, so I sent you a postcard. Did you get it yet?"

"No. But, listen, on the day we were selling totes and Duff—"

"I'm out of the tote business, Mary Mess-Up, and I want to stay out of it. Capisce?"

"Yeah, I capisce," I say. "You're not even around, so it will be easy to keep you out of it."

What happens next is that I am only a little wrong about that.

Once I know that the riding-lesson idea was a lie, I figure I might as well go back to my other plan and try to sell more totes. The next day I set up the table on the sidewalk again and put out the four Number Two Totes that are left. Maybe by now Mrs. Fufetti's friends have gossiped enough about Number Two Totes that I'll be able to sell some more.

I don't know if she told any of her friends, but I do know she told her nephew. That's because he walks up and introduces himself. "I'm Dan Thompson. My Aunt Susie told me all about you."

"I don't know any Aunt Susie," I say.

"She has Ceci? The poodle?"

"Oh! Mrs. Fufetti," I say. What I think is that Mrs. Fufetti must be *really* old if her nephew is already a grown-up.

"Yes. She told me about these Number Two Totes you're making. I was wondering where you got the idea and how you made them."

"I just came up with it," I say. "My big brother JT actually did the sewing because my mom won't let me use the sewing machine by myself and she's too busy being pregnant to help me."

Mr. Thompson is scribbling like crazy in his notebook. "So your brother helped you out. That's nice of him."

Shoot! I am not supposed to tell anyone about JT sewing. And I did tell, just like JT thought I would. Making that mistake makes me nervous and, before I know it, I'm doing that fast-talking thing again.

"But JT does not like to sew," I blurt out. "No sir-ee! He just does it as a favor to me. I'm eight. Actually, I'm almost nine. But my mom won't let me use the sewing machine. JT is thirteen. He hates to sew. Hates it! Says it's not his thing. Other things are his thing. Like he has his own Web site—Jtcity.com. *That's* his thing. And it's a very cool thing. You can go there and help build a pretend city. You can build schools. And a downtown with parks and everything. Go there sometime. I'm not kidding! JT would really like it if you would. In fact, he would really like it if a lot of people would go there. Because right now no one ever goes there. Not ever. Uh-uh. Never-ever."

"Whoa," Dan Thompson says. "Slow down."

I'm glad that he stopped me because I was just about out of breath. "That's what my brother tells me, too," I say.

He laughs.

"I'm a reporter for the *Sunnydale News*," he says. "I'm doing an article about unusual things kids are doing on their summer vacations. I'd like to include you and your Number Two Totes. Could I interview you—ask you a few questions about your Number Two Tote business?"

"You mean I would be in the newspaper?" I say.

"Yes, but not for another week."

"So that would be kind of like being famous, right?"

"Famous around here," he says. "Now what about your brother?"

"Him? He's at camp."

"Well, I suppose I wouldn't have to interview him," Mr. Thompson says. "I could just write about how he's involved without actually quoting him."

UH-OH! I think to myself. "Oh, no, you can't," I say. "You definitely cannot put JT in the newspaper. I promised him I would never tell anyone! It was the only way he would help me. Telling you was an accident. JT does not want his friends to know that he sews. If he found out that I told, he would, he would . . ."

"Don't worry," Mr. Thompson says, laughing. "I understand. I won't say anything about JT."

Which is a fib. Because he actually says quite a bit about JT.

11. Crash on a Scooter

Number Two Totes Stylish Solution for Pets Answering Nature's Call

by Dan Thompson

"In many ways, Mary Margaret Anderson is a typical eight-year-old. She likes to ride her scooter and swim. She can't wait to turn nine. She loves all animals, but especially dogs and hopes to have one of her own someday," my dad reads, when the paper comes a week later.

"She also has a lot of big ideas. 'I get ideas from all over the place,' she says. 'They just pop into my head, and sometimes I can't get them to leave until I do whatever I'm thinking of.'

"Her latest idea is a reusable fabric bag for carrying—how can we say this delicately?—a dog's business. 'We thought about calling them poop purses, but my mom didn't think it was very civilized . . .'"

"Oh, Mary Margaret," groans my mother. "Did you have to?"

"Sh-sh-sh," my dad says.

"'. . . so we call them Number Two Totes,' she says. 'You still use disposable plastic bags to pick IT up, but then you drop the bag right into the tote until you find a trash can.' The Number Two Totes come in leopard print, tie-dye spandex, and red velvet. 'I tried to pick material that most people would like,' she says.

"Miss Anderson, who is a bit of a fashion maven, got the idea from watching people walk their pets to the park. 'The owners always look good,' she says. 'Their outfits always match, but they were carrying these plastic see-through bags that were plain ugly. And then when my mom was looking through a catalog of baby stuff, I saw baby bottles that have disposable liners. The two things— the ugly plastic bags and the disposable liners— banged into each other in my brain. That's how I got the idea for Number Two Totes.'

"Family members help her with various aspects of the business. (In fact, creativity seems to run in the family. See New and Newsworthy *on page B6.)"*

Uh-oh. What is that all about, I wonder.

"According to Miss Anderson, interest has been high, but sales, which she conducts from the sidewalk in front of her house on Park Street, haven't exactly been brisk. She doesn't seem to mind. 'I can be patient,' she says

cheerfully. 'I've been waiting for a pet all summer, so this is not a big deal.'"

I try not to, but I get a big smile on my face at that last part. I was hoping he would put that in the article.

My mother raises one eyebrow at me, but she smiles, too. "You are my clever girl," she says.

"Very nice!" says my dad. "I'm proud of you."

I'm enjoying all the attention until I remember that JT, who is still at camp, might not feel proud of me at all. "Read the other part," I say to my dad. "The thing on page six."

Dad turns a few pages. "Here it is. 'New and Newsworthy. Bob Sloan won a blah, blah, blah, Erin McRobert, hmm-hmmm-hmmm.' Here!"

Created by thirteen-year-old JT Anderson, jtcity.com is a site where visitors can build a virtual city together. According to the site, "Sure, you can build your own virtual city by yourself, but how real is that? Real cities are built by lots of people. Real people. Sometimes they agree, and sometimes they don't. I've picked the scenario, but the rest is up to you and other visitors to this site. Join my experiment, and let's see what happens!'"

"Oh, thank you, Mr. Thompson," I blurt out.

"That's sweet of you, Mary Margaret—to be glad that JT was included in the paper, too," says my mother.

"Sure I'm glad," I say. Mostly about where he *wasn't* included.

That night, I write Andy another postcard.

Dear Andy,

Guess what? I was in the newspaper for Number Two Totes. A high school girl who is visiting from France saw the article and came and bought a leopard-print one. But she didn't even have a dog with her, so I don't get why she bought one. Anyway, I hope you're having fun at camp and that you made a friend. Hey, remember what my dad said? That people love talking about themselves? He's actually one hundred percent right about that! When the newspaper man asked me about myself, I blabbed everything—even about JT helping with the sewing. But it all worked out okay. I've been having fun with Itzy, but I miss you.

That last sentence kind of surprises me, but I wrote it, so it must be true. Andy was right that I didn't need him to sell Number Two Totes, and I don't even need him so that I can be close to his dog. But I do miss him.

Everyone always says that summer flies by, but my summer crawls by after that. I not only miss Andy, I also miss JT and want him to come home. I miss playing checkers or just hanging out on the front porch with him. I miss hearing his *click-click-click*ing on the computer. I even miss the way he changes my name. I don't always know what the words mean—like last Halloween when he called me Mary Macabre—but at least it's interesting.

And even being kind of famous in my town for a few days doesn't help. Because lots of people tell me they read about me and the Number Two Totes in the paper, but besides that French girl, nobody buys one. So after all that excitement, I spend a lot of time just hanging around the house and yard, reading and drawing and looking at bugs. Mostly I just feel floaty. I feel like Not-Me. Which means I don't feel like me. And our family doesn't feel like our family. And it has been a long, long time since my mom felt like my mom.

On one of the days, I mope around behind her while she talks on the phone and sweeps the floor. I follow her to her bedroom, where the baby is going to sleep when it finally gets here. I sit down on the floor and watch her arrange baby stuff. She lines up boxes and jars on the changing table. She stacks tiny diapers on a shelf. After she puts in teeny T-shirts and itty-bitty socks, she takes a step backward—and steps right on me.

"Ouch!" I say, louder than I need to, because that's the kind of mood I'm in.

Mom jumps. "Oh! I didn't see you back there," she says. "I'm sorry! What in the world are you doing?"

"Nothing."

She looks back at the changing table. "Hmm. Something is not quite right here," she says. Then she takes everything off the shelf.

"Mama."

Nothing. She's putting the socks in first this time.

"Llama-mama."

She doesn't even smile. Now she's putting in all the diapers.

"Llama-mama-pajama!"

"Oh, yes!" she says, but not to me. "I *should* put the pajamas next."

"Mom!"

Finally she turns around and sees me. "What? What is it?"

"I feel funny."

She puts her hand on my forehead. "You don't feel feverish. Do you think you have to throw up?" Even if everything else in my life is wobbly, I can still count on my mom to ask me this question. Which is kind of nice, actually.

"No. Not sick-funny. Strange-funny. I feel Not-Me."

She sits down in the rocking chair. "Me, too."

"You feel Not-Me, too?"

"Yes. Actually I feel Twice-Me, which is the same as feeling Not-Me, only it's bigger."

"Maybe I'll pick Not for the baby's middle name," I say.

"Let's test it," my mom says. "What if the first name were Robert? Robert Not Anderson. Or Caroline? Caroline Not Anderson. Hmmm. Maybe it will grow on me." She brushes my hair out of my eyes. "What would help you feel you?"

I think about this for a minute. "JT coming home. And a real pet, of course."

She sighs. "Oh, Mary Margaret. *Still* a pet?"

"Mrs. Fufetti says a pet is good for what ails you."

"She does? I'll have to remember to thank her for saying so the next time I see her," my mom says. "If only you could wait—"

"Wait? I *have* waited! All summer! You said you would do what you could, remember?"

"Now be fair," she says. "You did have ants."

"But that didn't count. They didn't *do* anything. They didn't even sleep."

"I told you that you'd have to be flexible."

I give up on her and just stomp off to my room then. The thing is, I am not sure how much more of this waiting and being flexible stuff I can take. It's not like I'm a grown-up or something. I'm not even nine yet. But my mom doesn't seem to get that.

Fortunately, JT does get it—or maybe he's still feeling bad about the trick he played on me—because a few days later, when we go to pick him up from camp, he has something for me. It is a *P-E-T* pet. In fact, it is a *T-U-R-T-L-E* turtle.

"His name is Crash," says JT. "I found him yesterday in our canoe. He reminded me of you—being someplace he didn't belong."

"Very funny," I say.

"Think you can handle taking care of him?" he asks.

"Of course I can," I say. "Just like I handled taking care of Brianna, Emma, Sarah, Jessica, Monica, Anna, Julia, and Frank."

"Didn't one of them die, though? Maybe we should re-think this." He's just kidding, though. "How do you re-member all their names, anyway?"

"That's easy. I just think of the poem I made up." I look at Mom. "Can I keep him?" I ask.

"I don't know," she says.

"That means don't get your hopes up," JT says.

"Please? Remember about me feeling Not-Me? And pets being good for what ails you?"

"Well . . . I suppose," she says. "But I'm counting on you to do everything yourself. Can I count on you?"

"Wee, wee," I say.

"*Wee?*" says JT.

"*Oui,*" says Mom. "It's French for 'yes.' She got that from a French exchange student who bought a poo—Num-ber Two Tote."

JT laughs, but I don't care. My mother has said yes, and I'm pretty sure that it still counts, even if she says it in an-other language.

"Thanks, JT. Thanks, Mom. You just made me about the happiest girl in the world!" I say from the backseat, where Crash and I are getting familiar.

"You're welcome," JT says, pulling on his seat belt.

"So how are you?" my mom asks JT. "How was camp this year? Did you get enough to eat?"

"Let's see. Tired. Different. And pretty much," JT says. "The food wasn't any better, though. Stew, Sloppy Joes, chili—it all looks and tastes the same. I think it's all the same food, but they just call it a different name each night."

My mom and I laugh, but thinking about JT eating at camp makes me think of Andy and how he was worried that he would have to sit by himself in the cafeteria. And then I wonder if maybe JT felt that way, too, since Duff hadn't been there with him.

"Did you miss anybody?"

"Like who? You?"

"No, like Duff or anything?" I ask.

JT looks away and out the window. "It was weird for a day or two, but I did all right," he says. "I met a few other people."

"Anybody special?" teases my mom.

JT doesn't answer that question. He just says, "So anything interesting going on at home? What did I miss?"

"Not that much," I say. "Just one thing, really." I shove the two newspaper articles into the front seat, between JT and Mom. "We got into the newspaper."

JT reads the article and then says, "Mystery Margaret, how did this reporter know about my site?"

"I told him."

"But how did my name even come up?"

"Ummm. I don't remember *exactly* how it came up," I say. "It just did. You know, the way things sometimes do during a normal conversation."

"So now everybody knows about jtcity.com?"

"Well, yeah," I say. "Everybody who reads the paper."

"Couldn't you just stick to blabbing about your own life?" he asks. "Just once?"

"For Pete's sake!" says my mom. "JT, what difference does it make? Aren't you pleased your site got into the paper?"

"Not really," he says. But when he hands the article back to me, I can tell that he's trying not to smile.

Mom says, "Well, Dad went to your site today, and more than three hundred visitors have been there. Some of them have been working on your pretend city, and it's huge."

"*Virtual*, Mom," JT says. "It's a virtual city, not a pretend city. It's huge, huh?"

"Hugely huge," says my mom.

And then JT does smile.

When we get home, the first thing JT does is to check jtcity.com. I am feeling happy because of Crash and because JT isn't mad at me anymore and because Andy will be home soon, so it's easy to be happy for JT, too. After watching JT look at his city and telling him (lots of times) how great his site is, I ask him to help me find out how to take care of turtles.

"Ask it what turtles eat," I say.

He types in a few words and then reads the screen. "Where can I find recipes for cooking with turtle meat?"

"Ugh! That's not what I want to know!"

JT is already clicking away again. "Wait. Here's something. 'Information about the animal the turtle.'" The Web site we go to tells me everything I need to know about how to take care of Crash all by myself. That's how I learn how often to change his water, and that I need to put a desk lamp over his bowl so he can get warm under the light, and that I should feed him twice a day. I wonder, though, if I should be feeding him more often because no matter how much I feed him, he gulps down his food like he is starving. But maybe he didn't know how to find food for himself in the wild and he's just making up for lost time.

We also have some fun, me and Crash. In our town there's a law that pets have to be on leashes, so I put a leash on him when we take our first walk together. Actually, it's just a piece of pink thread that I tie around his neck, which is not easy to do because he keeps pulling his head in. So I only do that once. I also put him in a basket and put the basket over the handlebars of the scooter and we scooter around the neighborhood together. He likes to go fast, just like me.

"How can you tell he likes to go fast?" my dad asks.

"Because he stretches his neck out as far as he can," I say. "Like he likes the feel of the wind."

"Maybe he's just scared stiff," my dad says. But I think I know my own turtle. Pet owners and their pets are very connected, almost like they share a brain. And I don't think Crash is scared.

By the time Andy comes home a few days later, I am dying to show him Crash, so I hang out in Andy's front yard and play with Itzy while I wait for him. When Andy's car finally drives in the driveway and he climbs out, I yell, "Hey, Andy! You'll never guess what I—"

But right then I see that he's wearing a shiny medal around his neck and a smile that's about as wide as my mom's belly.

He holds up the medal. "I won," he says. "I won the camp competition!" And before I can even get over there to say "Congratulations," he's blurting out everything about how he went to camp and didn't know anyone, but he remembered to ask the other campers about themselves, and pretty soon he had a few friends. And he wasn't the worst player there at all, and over the two weeks he got a lot better by practicing even more than he does at home. But he didn't know how much better until the competition, when he played the best he had ever played *in his life* and won.

And it's weird because I don't even mind waiting to tell him all about Crash. Instead, I feel happy right along with him when he tells me about winning the medal. I can imagine what it must have been like for Andy when the judge put the warm gold medal around his neck and everyone in the auditorium clapped for him so loud and so long that the stage started to vibrate and he was sure all that clapping would vibrate him right off the stage. I can see it all. Just like I was there on the stage with him, even though I wasn't.

12. Ruby the Polite Pig

There's not much of the summer left once Andy gets home. I'm glad I have Andy and Crash and Itzy to play with, because Mom and Dad are spending their last weeks before the baby comes shopping, cleaning, and organizing everything in sight.

JT is spending more time on the computer than ever. He says he's busy with jtcity.com, which is getting bigger every day. But I know for a fact that sometimes he also does instant messaging with a friend from camp—Casey. That's only because I happened to be walking by once when those two were IM'ing, which is not exactly snooping because JT was right there. And I know for a fact that she's a girl because she's in one of his pictures from camp and she's wearing a necklace with big gold letters that spell *C-A-S-E-Y*.

JT might be thinking of *C-A-S-E-Y*, but the end of summer makes me think of something else: *B-I-R-T-H-D-A-Y*. Mine. It's a tradition that we spend part of Labor Day weekend at my grandparents' farm, and my birthday usually happens right around Labor Day. I'm looking forward to it and so is my grandpa, who calls me to make sure we're coming.

"I understand you finally got a pet!" he says. "How's that turtle?"

"My friend's dog, Itzy, almost ate him yesterday," I say.

"Great!" he booms. *Great?* Sometimes my grandpa doesn't listen that well.

"Say," he says. "Grandma and I were thinking about your birthday. You're all coming again this year, aren't you?"

"Yes! I can't wait!"

"That's the best part of a birthday, isn't it?" he says.

"What?"

"The *anticipation*," he says. "Looking forward to it! That's why I want to give you a few clues about your present."

"I love clues, Grandpa. But you better be careful because I'm pretty clever and I might figure it out."

Grandpa doesn't say anything.

"Grandpa? Are you still there?"

"Yes, but I'm thinking. I'm thinking about what clues I want to give you. Okay, here they are. One: It's alive. Two: It starts out small. And three: If you take care of it, it grows!"

"Really?"

"Yep. And it's not too far from where I'm standing right this minute. So just think on *that!*" He chuckles. "But let's just keep these between the two of us, okay? I don't want anybody helping you figure it out."

"Would it be all right if I told Crash?"

"Sure," he says. "But no other family members."

As soon as I get off the phone, I tell Crash all about Grandpa's clues. When I ask Crash to guess what the present it, he just looks up at me. I have to say that he is a good listener, though.

Crash isn't perfect, but I do like having him and I am good at taking care of him.

"He seems like a perfect pet for this home," my mom says one day.

But then we find out that he definitely isn't.

Crash is a snapping turtle, which is why he snaps up all his food like he's starving. And the bigger he gets, the harder he is going to bite.

JT gets back on the Internet. "Snapping turtles are predators," he reads. My mother frowns. "They are extremely ravenous. They will eat anything they catch." My mother crosses her arms and lays them on the top of her stomach, which is so big that she can put a cup and a plate on it—just like having her own snack tray.

"Snapping turtles cannot hide completely in their shells. Their snapping jaws are a way of defending themselves," reads JT.

My mother closes her eyes and shakes her head.

Crash, as my brother says, is history.

We put Crash in a box and take him to a nature center close by.

"Maybe we can find a box turtle," says JT.

He's trying to be nice, but to tell the truth I don't want any kind of turtle. I could hold Crash, but something still wasn't right. When Itzy licks my face, I feel happy. When Grandpa's three-legged barn cat, Eileen, sits in my lap and purrs, I feel warm inside. But when Crash blinks at me, I don't feel anything.

I am sad on the drive home. The ants weren't real pets, and neither was Crash. And those Number Two Totes turned out to be not that popular, so I probably will never be able to save enough money to buy a dog and keep it in a kennel. Things are not looking good for me.

"You're awfully quiet, Mary Margaret," says my mom. "Are you thinking about Crash?"

"No, I'm thinking about how long it will take me until a Plan X to get a *real* pet."

"Plan X?"

"Yeah. You know. Plan A, B, C? There's a hundred and ten percent chance that it will take me until Plan X. I'll probably be ninety-three by then."

"Speaking of getting older," she says, "we'll be going to the farm soon to celebrate someone's birthday."

I know what she's trying to do. She is trying to make me forget about Crash. And it works. Because right then I remember the clues that Grandpa gave me. My present is something that starts out small and grows *and* it is something alive. Which means it must be some kind of pet.

When I get home, there's a message on the machine from Andy asking me if I'd like to go to Great America with him and his family the weekend after schools starts. I ask my mom and she says I can, so I call him back to tell him.

And then I tell him all about what my grandpa said and what I think it means.

"What kind of pet do you think it is?" he asks.

"I don't know," I say. "There's his barn cat, Eileen. But cats have dander, so it can't be her."

"What were the clues again?"

"It's alive, it starts out small, and it grows. Oh! And he said it's close to him."

"So maybe it's a baby something," Andy says. "What other animals does he have?"

"Nothing besides Eileen. He sold all the cows a few years ago to his neighbors, who also have some pigs." And then I gasp. "Andy, I know what it is. It's a baby pig."

"Gee, Mary Margaret. I don't know," says Andy. "A pig in the city? Aren't there laws against that?"

I'm not listening, though. I'm thinking that baby pigs are little and they don't have much hair, so they probably don't have dander. "Andy, I'm getting a warm, soft baby pig for my birthday!"

"Are you sure?"

"Absolutely. I gotta go, Andy. I have to get things ready for Ruby."

"Who's Ruby?"

"My pig, of course."

I love the farm because I can explore by myself and I can be as loud as I want and no one tells me to shush. I can weed the garden or dig in the dirt or pick peas or beans, and even though my mom always says, "Try to stay just a little clean, Mary Margaret," she knows I won't and she doesn't even mind that much.

The very first thing I do when I get there this time is hug my grandpa and grandma. My grandpa winks at me. I wink back and push the tip of my nose up with my finger to let him know I have guessed what my present is. He just laughs and says, "Better be careful, or your face will freeze that way." But I know for a fact that's not true.

Then I walk around the farm, wondering where Ruby might be. Eileen the cat sees me before I see her. She hobbles over to me and winds through my legs. I squat down. "Have you met Ruby?" I whisper in her ear. She shakes her head.

After I give up on finding Ruby, which I do pretty fast because I don't want to spoil my own surprise, I go out to the cornfield and look for bugs under rocks. Then I watch the monarch butterflies in the hayfield. I make up a hello song right on the spot and sing it to them.

"Hello, monarch butterflies,
Wings spread out against the sky.
What's it like up there so high?
Do bugs ever hit you in the eye?"

Then I think for another minute and add:

"Like when I ride my bike?"

I catch one and look at it for a little while. Then I let it go and sing a good-bye song.

"Good-bye, monarch butterfly.
Which is better, March or July?
Which is better, cake or pie?
If you can't decide, then it's a tie."

That's all I do all afternoon. And because I know that later I'll be getting a pet, it is a perfect afternoon.

At night we have my party. My birthday cake is a pumpkin pie because that's what I picked when I was three and ever since then it's been a tradition. I squinch my eyes up tight and make a wish. I blow out all nine candles and I know I'm going to get my heart's true wish—a real pet. I know it and Grandpa knows it. All summer I have been patient, I have been flexible, and I have been responsible. I took good care of the ants, even though ants aren't that much fun; and I took good care of Crash, even though he turned out to be a snapping turtle. Today I am going to get my just reward.

My dad puts four presents down on the table. None of them *looks* like a baby pig. When I can't figure out which one is from Grandpa, I open the one that's closest to me. It's *The Big Book of Wild Animals* from my grandma. "Remember when we saw paw prints out in the field?" Grandma asks. "That book tells you what each animal's paw print looks like. It tells other things, too. It will come in handy on our nature walks."

"Thanks, Grandma," I say. "I like it!" Because I do.

I open the second one. It's a water bottle for my bike from JT. "Just like the one I have," he says.

"Thanks, JT," I say. "I'll use this a lot." Because I will.

The third one is a new backpack from my mom and dad. "You always say your old one is too small," my dad says. "This one has lots more room."

"Thank you," I say. "Now I can check out even more library books!"

There is still one present to go—the present from Grandpa. I open it very slowly. Inside is a pair of rubber boots. *Rubber boots?* I think. "Gee, thanks," I say. My eyes get hot and watery. I don't understand. Grandpa said my present would be something alive, but any kid knows that boots are not alive.

He laughs and then says, "Oh, Mary Margaret. That's not everything. Those are just something you're going to need for *this*." He hands me an envelope.

I open it and read the note inside out loud.

"This birthday present to you from me
Requires some responsibility.
Feed it, water it, tend it well.
Watching it grow will be just swell.
I have no doubt that you're up to the task.
Mary Margaret, you're nine at last!"

Now I get it. I am going to need the boots to take care of my pet! "Thank you, Grandpa! Oh, thank you!" I give him a big hug.

He laughs. "Well, I was a better farmer than I am a poet. Don't you want to see what it is? Follow the string!"

"This is the best birthday ever!" I say. "I will never forget it!"

I follow the string out the door. It leads past the flower garden, then around the big oak tree with the rope swing, and up to the barn. That's where Ruby must be, I think. But the string doesn't end there. "Keep going, Mary Margaret!" says Grandpa.

Finally, the string ends at a cardboard box next to the first row of beans in the garden. Ruby must be in that box. I don't hear any grunts or snorts coming from the box, but maybe Ruby is a very quiet, polite pig.

I peek in and see . . . packets of seeds.

"But where's the p—?"

"Peas?" my grandpa asks. He grins. "Well, Mary Margaret. They are in there. Right along with the carrots and beans. That's right! Next summer you get to have your very own garden! That's why I wanted to keep it a secret. Your mom doesn't like you to get too dirty, but those boots should help you stay clean."

"Thanks," I say.

He thumps my back and gives me a bear hug. "You are welcome. I knew that this would be the perfect gift for you."

Everyone oohhs and ahhs over the packages of seeds

for a few minutes. On our way back to the house, Grandpa says to me, "Only a few weeks before you're a big sister. What do you think about that baby coming?"

Over the summer, a bazillion people have asked me this question, so I've gotten good at answering it. Usually I say, "I'm excited." And it's true that I am excited, that I can't wait until the baby comes out because when it does the hormones that make my mom cranky will come out, too, and then I will get my mom back the way she was.

Usually I say I'm excited, but right now I'm so full of being disappointed that I say, "Who cares about that dumb baby! This is *my* birthday. It's my worst birthday ever, and I will never forget it!" I bust out crying. I can't help it, and once I start I can't stop. I don't even want to stop.

My grandpa tries to put his arm around me, but I twist away. "Hey, hey, hey," he says. "Come on, now. Do nine-year-olds cry?"

"THIS ONE DOES!" I yell. I run to the barn.

Eileen is there. I lie down in the hay beside her and cry and cry. I cry because Grandpa said—well, almost said—that I was getting a pig. And all I got was stupid seeds. I cry because I did everything right and I still don't have a real pet. I don't even have my old kiki to help me feel better. And I cry because I've only been nine for a day and I already hate it because as far as I can tell, nine is not old enough to have a pet but too old to cry.

Dad finds me. "Hi, Sweetness," he says, sitting down in the hay next to me.

But I don't feel like a sweetness.

"What you said to Grandpa wasn't very nice."

"I know."

"I think you're disappointed about something."

I nod and blubber, "I thought the p-p-present was going to be a baby pi-ig. I was going to name it Ruby."

He hands me a Kleenex. "A baby pig? Why did you think that?"

"Because Grandpa told me on the phone it was a living thing that was close by him. There are pigs next door." I sniffle and wipe my nose. "And then the note said feed it. It said water it. It said it would grow. A baby pig needs food and water. It grows."

He sighs. "I know it's hard when you expect one thing and then get something else."

"It's not fair," I say. I feel flat and limp, like a balloon that all of the air has gone out of.

"You're right; it's not."

"I know I'm right."

"Don't worry. Things will work out somehow. They always do." He picks some hay out of my hair. "Do you feel like coming back to the house?"

"I don't think so."

"Okay. Maybe you will in a little while."

"Maybe."

"Don't forget," he says. "Tonight you get to stay up later." Then he leaves.

I pet Eileen for a long time. She lies back and purrs for

a while; then she sits up and starts cleaning herself, licking the stump where her leg used to be. I think it must be easier to be Eileen and have only three legs than to be nine and not get the thing you wanted more than anything else on your birthday.

When the sun goes down, I go back to the house. Grandpa is waiting for me on the porch swing and I sit down beside him. "Mary Margaret, your dad told me everything," he says. "I'm sorry your present wasn't what you expected. When I gave you those hints, I didn't even think that you would be thinking about pets. You already had one—Crash."

"It's okay," I say. "I'm sorry, too. For what I said."

He holds out his hand. "Buddies?"

"Buddies," I say, taking it.

Grandma and Mom and Dad are all outside, too, sitting in lawn chairs and talking quietly. Together, we wait for the deer to come out of the woods to eat in the hayfield.

"How do you spell Ruby?" I ask.

"R-U-B-Y," Grandpa says. "Why?"

"Because that's what I want for the baby's middle name. But Dad said no four-letter words."

"I think Ruby would be just fine," my mom says. "Ruby it is. Whether the baby is a boy or girl."

"Good," I say. Then I watch the fireflies sparkle in the dark and listen to the urrr-eeets of the crickets. I think about how Dad said things will work out somehow. The thing is, I don't know how.

13. Meltdown at the Mall

By the time we get back to our town Labor Day it's late, but we stop on the way home to go shopping for school clothes. My dad asks JT what he needs and JT says, "Just jeans and T-shirts—should be pretty easy. Unlike shopping for dude duds."

"For what?" my mom asks.

"Dude duds—the kind of clothes that the guys Duff is hanging out with wear," he says. "And Duff, too. Not that it matters to me. He can wear what he wants."

"Maybe once school starts, you'll all be friends," she says.

JT looks over at me and rolls his eyes, which means "Mom doesn't get it," and that makes me feel good because it means he thinks that I do get it. "I don't think so," he says.

My dad and JT head to the men's department. "See you in an hour," Dad says. "Have fun, ladies."

I think that the chances for that are about zero, since I am not in the mood to be cheered up.

Inside the store, my mom holds up a blue skirt.

"No," I say. "No skirts."

"No harm in trying," she says. She puts it back.

She holds up pink leggings. I shake my head. "Negatory."

"*Negatory?*"

"That means no," I say.

"I know what it means," she snaps.

"I'll take those zebra-striped leggings, though," I say.

"You can have those if you'll agree to this." She holds out a white T-shirt.

"Isn't that a little . . . ordinary?"

"This is a deal-breaker," she says. "No white shirt, no zebra leggings."

"Okay, deal," I say. I can always wear something over the T-shirt to spark it up a little.

She pulls a pair of corduroys off a shelf.

"Too line-y," I say.

"That is not a very good reason," she says. "They are supposed to be line-y." But she puts them back on the shelf.

Next she points to a plaid sweater on the shelf. "*Very* fashionable," she says.

I hold it up to my face and look in the mirror, then hand it back to her.

"What's wrong with it?" she asks.

"It clashes with my freckles."

"But the zebra leggings *don't* clash with your freckles?"

"That's right," I say. "They don't." I might have to shop with my mother, but I don't have to make it easy for her.

She sighs. "Okay, Mary Margaret. *You* pick something."

I find a pair of yellow suede pants that have fringe up the sides.

"Fine," she says. She is so huge with that baby that she waddles when she goes up to the counter to pay for the clothes. By the time we are out of the store we are both tired. Mostly of each other.

"Maybe it's time for you to go back to school," she crabs when she packs her enormous self into our van and slams the door.

Before I open the door to the back, I say, "Maybe it's time for you to have that baby," because I think she can't hear me through her closed door.

Except that her window is down and she hears me. "Mary Margaret! What did you say?"

This is what JT would call a tight spot. "I said . . . maybe it's time for you to havataby."

"What's *havataby?*"

I kick my brain right in the behind to come up with a good answer. "It's French for a getting a good night of sl—"

"No. Stop right there," my mom says. "Don't you try to talk your way out of this. You said, 'It's time for you to have that baby.' That was backtalk, and I won't have it! You've just lost the privilege of . . . of . . . of going with Andy to the amusement park!"

"Fine with me! It's been so *fun* at home, who needs the amusement park?" I say, because I can't seem to stop myself. "Stupid ants and a snapping turtle for pets. I guess I really *am* the luckiest girl alive."

"Listen, young lady! Enough is enough."

Suddenly I realize that she's right. Enough *is* enough. And I have too much enough inside of me. There is so much enough inside me that even though I am nine and bigger than I was when I was eight, I am not big enough to hold it all, and it springs right out of me. All that extra enough pulls my new clothes out of the bag and throws them on the ground. And stamps on them, because . . . well, I don't know why, but it does.

By now my mom has rolled herself out of the van and waddled back over to me. "Stop!" she says, putting her hands on my shoulders. "What's wrong?"

"Everything!" I yell. I wriggle away from her and give the ordinary white T-shirt a final stomp. "Everything is wrong. Lester, and the ants, and Crash, and JT and—and—and"—but I can't finish.

"And what?"

"You! *You're* all wrong." And I think my mom will be mad that I said it, but I don't care. It's the truth and I'm glad I said it. But when I look at her, she is not standing angry with her hands on her hips. She is standing sad, with saggy shoulders and tears in her eyes, and then I'm not glad I said it. I feel like I do after I stub my toe—like if I could just take that one second back I would be so much more careful, but it's too late for that because once you stub your toe, you can't unstub it. You just have to wait for the pain to go away.

When my mom doesn't say anything, I say, "All I want is

the old you so that I can be the old me. I want us to be the way we were before."

"Before what?"

"Before this summer. Before . . . before . . . *that*," I say, pointing at her belly. "I wish that baby wasn't there." And once I've said that, I suddenly feel light and free, like I do after I've been pulling Jolene around in the wagon and she gets out halfway around the block. I still have to pull the wagon home, but it's so much easier.

My mom sighs. "I think I knew you were feeling this way all along," she says. "I've just been so tired and preoccupied, and I guess I was hoping it would all work out on its own."

She looks at me like she's waiting for me to say something, but I'm temporarily out of words, so she keeps going. "I know all this is hard on you, because you are used to being center stage in our family. I won't lie to you. Even after I have the baby, I won't be the way I was before. I'll be back to my normal size—at least I hope I will—but we're going to have a new little person to love and take care of. We're going to make room for that person, just like Dad and I and JT made room for you when you came along. We're going to love this baby because the baby is part of us."

"It's not a part of me," I say. "Besides, our family is already full."

"That's the great thing about families, Mary Margaret. They are never full. Remember your birthday pie?"

"Sure. There were just enough pieces for all of us, because Grandpa and I had seconds. That's what I mean—there's no room for another person."

"I'm talking about the candles. When you light the ninth birthday candle, the first eight still burn. Love is like the flames on the candles. You can light as many as you want. It's not like a birthday pie that you run out of. It's like candles—you can always light one more."

"Andy's the only candle in his family," I grumble. "Plus he has a dog."

"That's Andy's family. This is our family. Besides, you might be surprised by how much you love the baby."

I doubt it. Because the problem with all that love-being-like-birthday-candles stuff is that you have to *want* to light that next candle. Mom and Dad might want to, and JT might not care one way or the other, but not me.

Too bad that I don't get to decide. It seems to me like if I can't decide whether or not to add someone to our family, I should at least be able to decide when the baby comes, but I don't get to decide that, either.

14. Back-to-School Campout

The very next day is the first day of school, and just when I am trying to decide what to wear now that I'm a fourth-grader, I overhear Mom telling Dad that she feels funny.

"Funny how?" Dad asks.

"I can't be sure, but I think labor-and-delivery funny," she says.

"I'll go call your parents," he says. "Just in case."

Later, when JT and I are eating our toast, Dad tells us that Grandpa and Grandma are coming. "They'll be here by the time you get home from school, just in case Mom and I end up going to the hospital today."

"I've changed my mind about having this baby," my mom says. "I'll just stay pregnant for the rest of my life."

"Mom, that's impossible!" I say. And then, just to be sure, I ask JT, "It is impossible, isn't it?"

"She's just nervous," says JT.

"I'm too old for this," my mom says.

"What are you talking about? You're just getting good at it," says my dad. "Besides, you'll have lots of help."

"Sure, I'll help," says JT.

"And you know I'll do whatever needs to be done," says my dad.

I don't say anything. I just put my plate in the sink and go brush my teeth.

When Andy rings the doorbell, I give my mom a hug good-bye. My arms don't fit all the way around her anymore, even when I stretch, but I do my best to hang on tight. I think about how we used to fit so well together when we hugged, but then she got fat with the baby and I grew a couple of inches and got all bony. She'll be skinnier again, but I'm still growing. What if we never fit together again?

Suddenly I feel the way I feel when Jessie and Jolene's mom gives me a ride home from swimming lessons. I know I'll get there, but everything will be different on the way. Our car always smells a little like pepperoni pizza. Their car smells like an old banana. We listen to jazz music. They listen to Sing-Along-Song Gang. We go home past the diner, the gas station, and the pink house. They go home past the post office, the library, and the pink house. *I'm* even different on the way home.

"Okay, Loverly. Time for you to be off," my mom says, pulling away. "Have a great first day of school." I want to give my mom something else. I look around the room and see an old picture of me and JT when I was about a year old. Actually, you can barely see JT in the picture because I was sticking my head right in front of his. JT says he should have known right then that I'd be an attention hog. I shove the picture at my mom. "Here. Take this," I say. "So you remember."

My mom doesn't ask me, "Remember what?" Instead, she smiles and uses her thumb to wipe a little dust off the picture. Then she bends over—as well as she can, which isn't very well, to tell the truth—looks me in the eye, and says, "Loverly, I'll remember." She stands up, slips the picture into her purse, and says, "See you later, alligator."

"After a while, crocodile," I say, wondering how I am going to be able to concentrate on school. Fortunately, the first day of school doesn't take much concentration. All we do is something my teacher calls "housekeeping," which sounds a lot like we'll be sweeping and dusting but turns out to be finding out where we sit and learning "the rules of the classroom." Which are pretty much the same rules that we had in last year's classroom.

When I get home from school, JT is up on a ladder, fiddling with one of the screens. Grandpa is holding the ladder and Grandma is saying, "JT, be careful! Are you sure this is a good idea?"

"What's going on?" I ask.

"Dad forgot to leave the extra house key," JT says. "We have to break in."

"Locked out? You mean we can't get in?" I ask. My voice

is high and squeaky, and suddenly I'm very hot. I know it's silly to be so upset, but I can't help it.

"Don't freak, Mary Margaret," says JT. "Everything is under control."

We have an old house with the kind of screens that fasten on the outside. Because the windows are open, all JT has to do is take a screen off a window, then climb through.

"Piece of cake," JT says, disappearing into the house. In another minute he's unlocking the front door for us.

We find a note from Dad on the counter, but it doesn't say much. Just that they went to the hospital, Mom's contractions are still pretty far apart, they'll call later and they love us. I picture Mom lying on the hospital bed. She hates having cold feet, so I hope she remembered her slippers. She doesn't like cuts or blood, either, so I hope that it doesn't hurt too much when she has the baby.

"There's a P.S.," says JT. "It says, 'Couldn't find the extra house key, but I left the door unlocked for you.'"

Grandma laughs. "Well, he *thought* he was going to leave the door unlocked," she says. "I guess he forgot in all the rush to get to the hospital."

JT and I help Grandpa and Grandma take their things to JT's room. "Mom says you can sleep here," JT says. "Sorry it's a little messy. I wasn't expecting that you'd be coming so soon."

"It's fine," says Grandma. "But where will you sleep?"

"Maybe on the couch in the office. Or since the weather

is nice enough, maybe I'll pitch the tent in the backyard and sleep there."

"Would your parents mind?" Grandma asks.

"Negatory on that," says JT. "I don't have any homework or anything. The first week of school is pretty low-key."

"JT, can I sleep out there with you?" I ask. "I don't have any homework, either."

"No," says JT.

"Why not?"

"You make up poems in your sleep, like

"My name is Mary Margar-PET,
(A name that's easy to forget).
My brother JT is smart and cool.
Unlike him, I often drool."

"I don't make up poems in my sleep!"

"But you do drool," he says.

"JT," Grandpa says. "I think it would mean a lot to Mary Margaret if she could, especially tonight. Would you mind, just this once?"

One thing about JT is that he knows when he's licked and once Grandpa asks him, JT is definitely licked. "All right," he says. Then he turns to me and says, "Come on, Mary-Your-Majesty. Apparently my new job is to serve you."

"What's that supposed to mean?" I ask.

"Never mind. I'll get the tent from the basement. You get the sleeping bags."

I get the sleeping bags. But we never get the chance to sleep in them.

After dinner it's still warm out, but windy, too, which makes it hard to set up the tent. I do my best to help JT because I know that he is not that excited about me camping out with him. I think he knows I'm trying because he's a little bit nicer to me once we are all settled in the tent, me in my puppy p.j.s and him in his sweatpants.

"It's weird, isn't it?" JT says, rolling out his sleeping bag. "The next time we see Mom and Dad, they'll be holding a baby—a baby that will be with us night and day, for-ev-er."

"Yeah. Really weird." The wind is making all kinds of scary noises and I wonder if I should dig out my kiki—just for tonight.

I guess I wonder that out loud without meaning to because JT says, "I remember when they brought that thing home—your kiki."

"You do?"

"Yeah. I wouldn't have minded them bringing home a blanket, except you were attached to it. You were really tiny. I think the very first name I called you was Mary Mouse. You were so small, and when you breathed through your nose, it sounded like a squeak. I didn't like you much."

"You didn't?" JT might tease me or get mad at me sometimes, but I know that deep down he likes me. I'm surprised that he ever felt any different.

"Mom and Dad were always saying things like, 'Be quiet, you'll wake the baby.' Baby, baby, baby. That's all I ever heard. You sucked up all the attention in the room, like a tiny vacuum cleaner."

"Oh. Sorry."

"It wasn't your fault. It's just what babies do."

"All babies?"

JT thinks about this. "Yeah, pretty much. But they grow out of it. Things change." He chews on his thumbnail and stares at his feet. "People change."

"Yeah. Mom got a lot bigger and crabbier."

JT stops biting his nail and laughs. "That's the truth. She was getting so big I thought she was going to bust right out of the house." He opens a bag of Chee•tos and starts eating them. "Why don't you go get us a couple of Cokes?"

"Don't tease me, JT. You know I'm not supposed to have Coke at night. It has caffeine."

He grins. "I didn't tell you the best part about having a new baby in the house. With Mom and Dad being so busy with the baby, you are going to get away with a lot more stuff, at least for a while. Sometimes they'll be so tired they won't notice that you're watching TV when you shouldn't be. Or they'll notice, but they'll be too tired to care. Those perks go away after about six months, but then there are some new ones. Like there's somebody younger than you that you can boss around."

Right in the middle of licking his finger he stops and

says, "Hey, I just thought of something. My forever is shorter than yours! Five more years and I'll be in college."

It's just as weird to think of JT living someplace else as it is to think of a new baby living with us. And thinking about him moving out someday doesn't exactly make me feel any better.

15. Rabbit Raid

When I come back from getting the Cokes, JT is reading his book. I try to concentrate on my book, but the wind is making the tent a very loud place. Scritching and scratching. Thwapping and snapping. Whoo-ing and woo-ing.

Scrrr-itch. Scriiiiiii-tch. "What's that?" I ask JT.

JT turns a page of his book. "Nothing."

I hear someone or something scrunching up a paper bag. "JT!" I whisper. "Someone is out there killing a paper bag!"

"You're nuts," he says. "Who would want to murder a paper bag? It's just the leaves. Would you settle down and read your book?"

"I'm trying, but I can't with all this noise." By nine o'clock, when I am supposed to put down my flashlight and go to sleep, I'm so jumpy I can't even think of going to sleep.

Suddenly I see an arm outside the tent reaching for me. "JT! Look! Look at that. Something's trying to grab me!"

JT looks up from his book. "What are you talking about?"

"See? Right there."

"That's just the shadow of the branch from the bush, Mary Scare-dy. Go to sleep."

I whisper to myself:

"Oh be quiet, old JT.
Read your book and let me be.
So what if I'm a little scared,
Maybe it helps me be prepared."

Then I pull on my tennis shoes.

"Now what're you doing?" JT asks.

"I think I'll sleep with my shoes on, just in case."

"Just in case what?"

"Just in case I need to get out of here—fast."

"We live in town. What, are you afraid a streetlight is going to attack you? Or maybe all the blades of grass are going to gang up on you?" JT laughs.

"You think you are so funny," I say.

"Yeah, I do," he says, picking his book up again.

"Well, *you're* wearing shoes," I say.

"I just haven't taken them off yet." He shakes his head. "Sheesh. I'm at a good part in my book, so if you can't relax and be quiet, then just go sleep in the house. I guess this is what I get for letting you have a Coke."

JT goes back to reading, but I keep hearing noises.

Scritching noises, right by my head, but on the other side of the tent. I roll out of my sleeping bag and into JT's side. "JT. I know something is out there!"

Before JT can answer me, we both hear something unzipping the flap door of the tent. Suddenly a hand shoots in, grabs JT by the foot, and starts dragging him out of the tent. JT yelps, "Get off!" and tries to pull his foot back, but the hand won't let go.

I grab the flashlight and start hitting the hand—hard. "Let go!" I shout, using the flashlight like a hammer. "LET GO!"

"Hey! Ouch!" says Duff's voice, and the hand lets go. Outside we hear laughing. JT dives out of the tent and crashes right into Mike and Kevin. I climb out after JT, just in time to see him stumble to the side of the tent. "What are you guys doing here?" he says.

Duff shines a flashlight in JT's face, and JT holds his hands up over his eyes. JT's face is blue-white, like my feet get in the winter when I go barefoot in the house and they get icy cold.

Duff keeps the light on JT's face, just lowers it a little. "Man, you were so scared," he says. I can't see Mike and Kevin's faces very well because of the dark, but I can see their sharp white teeth.

JT kind of shrinks himself up into his sweats and hunches his shoulders. He presses his lips together.

The flashlight creates strange shadows that make Duff and his friends look like aliens. I still feel jumpy, the way I feel before I run a race in gym class. The flashlight is still in my hand and now I shine it on Duff. I do what I always do when I'm nervous. I talk.

"Where have you been, anyway?" I ask. "Our cookie jar has been empty for*ever*. Mom and I tried to make those no-bake cookies? We tried to do them just like you showed us, but the chocolate was too lumpy or something and they turned out awful! So could you show us how again? Not right now, I mean. It's a little late to start on cookies now. Although, you know what? That's a great idea! We could do it now. The kitchen would smell all good, just like it used to when you'd—"

"You make cookies?" Kevin says with a snort.

"Oh, yeah. Darryl's the man," Mike says. "The big man. Don't be messing with him, or he'll roll you out and put you in the oven."

Duff gives me a dirty look and JT hisses, "Shut up," but as he does, he bumps up against my arm and I drop the flashlight. When I reach down to pick it up, I see something furry in the grass right next to the tent. Then I hear that noise again. *Scritch-scritch-scritch*. I shine my flashlight along the tent and see that it's a rabbit, but something is wrong with it. When it tries to move, one of its paws rubs against the tent. That's what's been making the scritching sound.

"JT, I told you something was out here!" I say. "Look!"

Duff pushes by me. "Let me see!" And before I can stop him, he scoops up the rabbit. "Oh, it's a wit-tle bun-ny wab-bit," he says, in an Elmer Fudd voice. He holds it up for his friends to see. "Isn't it cu-ute?"

"You're squishing it! Give it back, Duff! I found it! It's mine."

"Not so fast, Mary Margaret," Kevin says. "Let's do an experiment."

Duff looks at Kevin. "What kind of experiment?" he asks.

"An experiment to find out if rabbits can swim."

"They can't," I say.

"Is that a fact or a hypothesis? I think you might be jumping to conclusions," Kevin says. Then he laughs. "Get it? *Jumping* to conclusions?"

"Rabbits can't swim, and you know it," says JT.

"I don't care if it can swim or not!" I say. "Just give it back to me."

"Oh, come on," says Mike. "We're just going to have a little fun with it."

"Let's use the pond at the park," says Kevin.

"Yeah. Let's go!" Mike turns and sprints toward the park. Duff watches him, then looks at us like he can't decide whether he should stay or go. Kevin elbows him in the ribs. "What are you waiting for? You got some brownies in the oven or something?"

"Nah, I'm ready," Duff says. He and Kevin take off after Mike.

"Don't worry," Kevin yells back to us. "We'll take care of this cu-te bun-ny wab-bit, girls." But I can tell by the way he says it that he won't.

"Wait!" JT and I shout at the same time.

JT turns to me. "I'm going to stop them. You stay here," he says.

"No! I'm coming, too!"

"We don't have time to fight about it!"

"Then let me come!" I shout, watching them disappear into the night. "Come on, JT!"

"No! This is *my* deal—not yours."

16. Mr. Tough Nose

I wait until I can't see him anymore, then I take off after him. I am running hard, panting, panting, panting; and my chest feels like it's going to bust open. I stumble and almost fall. I want to stop, but I think of the rabbit. I have to save the rabbit from Darryl, who was Duff but is not anymore, and so I keep going, hoping that JT is already there, stopping them.

Suddenly I can see them all again, up ahead of me at the edge of the pond, yelling at each other, but I can't hear what they are saying. When I get there, Mike has the rabbit.

"Don't do it!" JT shouts.

"Who is going to stop me?" Kevin says, laughing. Then he sees me. "Little girl, you should get a man for a brother instead of *this*," he says, pointing to JT.

All that being mad and frustrated and *disappointed* that boiled out of me when I had that fight with my mom is suddenly right back inside of me. Nobody calls me a little girl. And nobody insults my brother. And besides all that, Duff and JT were best friends and somehow these two dudes ruined it. Now it's time for them to pay.

I pull my arm back so I can sock Kevin in the stomach, but JT must have eyes on the side of his head because he grabs me hard by the wrist. And then he puts his face so close to mine that I can smell the Chee•tos on his breath and says in a tone I have never heard him use before, "I told you to stay out of it."

"But I can help."

"Oh, bringing in the big guns, huh, JT?" Mike says. "Go ahead. Let your little sister take her best shot."

JT's grip on my wrist tightens as he says, "I don't want your help."

"Fine, be stupid about it!" I shout. I jerk my hand away and step back, just in time to see Mike toss the rabbit to Duff, who catches it and then holds the rabbit high in one hand, where JT can't reach it. JT grabs Duff's other arm and says something to him—something none of the rest of us can hear. Duff tries to shake JT off, but JT won't let go.

Duff yells, "BACK OFF! Just BACK OFF!" But JT doesn't. He may be small, but he's strong in his own way.

Mike moves in and says, "No time for a chat. Let's do it!" And then he wrenches JT off Duff, who stumbles and starts to fall. I can't really tell what happens next because everyone's arms and legs are all mixed up together like a tumbleweed of people, and they all go down. Once they are down, they start grunting and wrestling.

Suddenly, I see the rabbit slowly hopping toward a

grove of trees. At first I'm happy for the rabbit, happy that it's free, but then I'm disappointed. I could've taken it home. It could've been the pet I always wanted. I can't catch it by myself, but maybe with JT's help . . .

JT groans and I realize that he's the one who needs my help, not the other way around. Kevin is twisting JT's arms behind his back and forcing him to his knees. It's three against one, and that's not even close to fair. I don't know what to do. I'm dying to barrel in there, slugging my guts out and kicking karate kicks. But I remember what JT said to me: *"Stay out of it."* How can I help him if I have to stay out of it? There must be another way besides getting in the middle of things. Like Dad says, I just need to think hard. Then it works again! *Grandpa and Grandma.*

I'm just about to turn and run to get them when Duff drags himself to his feet and stands right over JT. "You don't know me!" he says, panting.

"I do know you," JT says. "I know you went too far when you were trashing Elise's house. But this is worse. This—this *throwing a rabbit into a pond*—is just mean. And you aren't mean. This isn't you."

Mike lightly slaps Duff's head. "So if you aren't Darryl, who are you? An alien? From Planet Bake-Me?"

"Shut up," Duff says to Mike. "Just shut up." And then he says to JT, "Maybe you're wrong, JT. Maybe this *is* me."

"Then good luck," JT says. "You'll need lots of it if you keep letting these morons do your thinking for you."

In the split second between when JT says that and what

comes next, I start to think that maybe JT doesn't need my help or even Grandma and Grandpa's. But then what comes next is that Mike socks JT right in the nose.

"Ow!" JT says. He slumps against Kevin, who lets go of his arm. JT rolls onto the grass and covers his nose. When he takes his hand away, there's blood on it and on his nose and upper lip. It's pretty gross, to tell the truth.

Duff drops to his knees beside JT. "JT! Are you okay? Does anybody have a Kleenex?"

Mike and Kevin don't move. It's like we've been playing freeze tag and they've been tagged and have to stay in the same place. They just stare at JT's bleeding nose like they can't believe it.

Just then the lights from a car sweep over us, and a car door slams. A minute later a police officer is walking toward us.

"Everything okay?" he says.

Finally, someone who can help us out here! I open my mouth to tell him exactly how *not* okay everything is here, but JT beats me to it.

"Officer," he says, and then he glances at Mike and Kevin. They look at him, then at the handcuffs on the policeman's belt, and then at each other. To me, Mike seems flat, like the stick people that I used to draw in kindergarten. I almost feel sorry for him because I remember when Rat Man came to our house that day and how I didn't know what JT was going to say then, just like Mike doesn't know what JT is going to say now. It must be even worse for

Mike because there's a policeman waiting to drag him away.

Finally, JT says, "Everything is fine. I just have a bloody nose. It's not the first time."

The officer stares at us, first at JT and Duff, then at Mike and Kevin. "You sure?"

"Yeah. It's just a bloody nose. No big deal. I could use a Kleenex, though."

The officer gets a few from his car and gives them to Duff, who hands a few to JT. "Don't you boys think it's about time to be getting home?" the officer asks.

"Yes, sir," says Kevin. "It certainly is. We're headed there right now. Darryl, you coming?"

Duff hands JT another Kleenex and shakes his head. "I don't think so."

"Suit yourself," Mike says. Then he and Kevin are gone.

"You need a ride home?" the officer asks us.

"Yes!" I say, because suddenly I'm exhausted.

Duff helps JT up and over to the police car. I climb in first, then JT. "Want to come?" he asks Duff.

"Do you want me to?"

"If you want. We could hang out at my house—if you want. Either way. It doesn't matter to me," JT says. The way he is looking everywhere except right at Duff makes me think that it really does matter, though.

I'm glad when Duff says, "Sure, okay," and climbs in, too.

It's a short ride home, and nobody says anything. The

officer drops us all off at our house. We say "Thanks" and "Good night" and scuff up to the house. JT and Duff are both busy with their noses. JT is pinching his and Duff is sniffling like he's coming down with a cold.

"All that sniffling is getting on my nerves," JT says to Duff. "Why don't you use one of those things?" he asks, pointing to the Kleenexes Duff is holding.

"You're not going to need them all?"

"Nah, I think I'm about done here."

Duff says, "Yeah, me, too. I'm done with all of that. Know what I mean?"

"Maybe," says JT. "You haven't exactly been easy to figure out."

"I guess I have been kind of a jerk."

"You said it, not me," says JT.

"I know. I'm sorry. It was weird, how all that went. Like things started happening and I couldn't, I don't know, *stop* them."

"You could stop yourself, though," JT says. "Maybe think for yourself before you do stuff."

Duff shrugs. "Yeah, I guess."

I feel kind of good right then. Because it looks like maybe JT and Duff will still be friends after all. And because even though I'm only nine and Duff is thirteen, back there in the park I did think for myself and I stopped myself from getting in the middle of things.

"Whatever happened to that rabbit, anyway?" JT asks me.

"It hopped away when you were falling all over each other," I say.

"Hopped? It must have just been stunned or something outside the tent. At least it didn't end up taking a dip. That's one lucky bunny."

Once we're inside, we tell Grandpa and Grandma everything. They're pretty surprised by what went on while they were watching reruns of *The Dick Van Dyke Show*. Mom and Dad wouldn't have been so calm about it, but Grandpa and Grandma are. Or maybe they are too old and tired to make a big deal out of it. Either way, JT and I get off pretty easy. Even though it's ten o'clock at night, Grandma makes us grilled cheese sandwiches because we're all starving. After that, Grandpa takes Duff home and JT and I get ready for bed.

JT comes into the bathroom when I'm brushing my teeth. "Listen, Mary Margaret," he says. "I know you were just trying to help me out back there. I'm sorry if I was mean to you."

"Oo didin hoff to squish my wrish," I say through a mouthful of toothpaste.

"I'm sorry about that, too," JT says. "I needed you to listen, to understand. The thing is, I'll be going to school with those guys for a long time. They aren't going to go away, so I need to figure out how to face them and still be myself. But I didn't have the time to explain all that. I don't think I even *could* have explained all that until now."

I spit and rinse. And then spit again, which is my favorite part of brushing my teeth. "What do you mean, face them and still be yourself?"

JT looks at me like he's trying to decide something. Finally he says, "Remember a few weeks ago, when you were snooping on my computer, and I got mad at you and set that trap?"

"Yeah, the chore trap. You were pretty mad."

"I was mad at you, but I was also mad at myself, and I think I took it out on you. Remember that day when you and Andy were trying to sell poop purses—"

"Number Two Totes," I say.

"Right, and Duff and Mike and Kevin were teasing you about them? I heard everything. When you called Duff a syrup head, that's when I knew for sure you had been on my computer. Anyway, I should have come out and stood up for you, but I didn't. I was afraid they'd think I was, I don't know, even more different from them than they already thought. So I stayed inside and didn't do anything. I was a coward. Tonight I wanted to be different."

"You were," I say.

"Thanks," he says, smiling a little.

"You got a big nose. That's how you're different!" I slug him in the arm. "Just kidding. You were really brave. You saved the rabbit. You even look like a hero."

"I do?" he says.

"Yeah, that nose makes you look like Mr. Tough Guy."

He looks at himself in the mirror, lifting up his chin. "Yeah, it kind of does," he says.

I give him a hug then because basically I like him a lot. "Mary Mushy, cut it out," he says. But he gives me a squeeze before he pulls back.

When Grandma comes in to say good night she says that Dad just called to tell us what's going on at the hospital. In all the excitement, I haven't thought once about the baby. Just when I'm feeling pretty good about not thinking about the baby, I realize that I haven't thought about my mom during that time, either.

"Is Mom okay?" I ask Grandma.

"Fine, honey," Grandma says. "She is going to the delivery room right this minute."

Which means: The baby is on its way.

17. This One's a Tosser

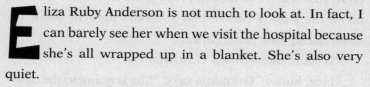

Eliza Ruby Anderson is not much to look at. In fact, I can barely see her when we visit the hospital because she's all wrapped up in a blanket. She's also very quiet.

"Hasn't complained a bit," says my dad.

"What a good baby," says my mom.

"She's a keeper," says the nurse.

On the way home I ask, "What does the hospital do with the babies that aren't keepers?"

"Oh, they are all keepers, Mary Margaret," says my dad.

It looks like the hospital was right. It looks like Baby Liza is not going to be much trouble, especially because Grandpa and Grandma stay for a few days to help out. Mom isn't exactly zippy right away, even though she isn't lugging that big ball of baby in her gut anymore. She doesn't take bike rides, but whenever she rests on the couch, she asks me to keep her company. Sometimes I bring along a book and read to her, but sometimes I just lie quietly on my side, with my back to her, so my head is tucked up under her chin, and match my breathing to hers, slow and steady. I have my mom back. My arms fit all the way around her again, and I think that maybe adding another candle to the family is no big deal.

I make up a poem and then read it to everybody:

"Tiny fingers, tiny toes,
Wrinkly face and tiny nose.
Tiny eyes are always closed.
Baby Liza sleeps the most!"

The first time Andy sees her, he says, "She's cute, in a wrinkly way. Kind of like those shar-pei dogs. It might be fun to have a little sister."

"It's more boring than having a dog," I say.

Because besides sleeping, all Liza does is eat and wet her diapers. Even when she's awake, all she does is look around and when that tires her out, she goes back to sleep. Day after day is pretty much the same. This new-baby stuff is going so well, I'll have a real pet in no time.

For a little while, there is just one small thing that bothers me. My mom starts calling the baby Lovey-Lou, which sounds a lot like Loverly, if you ask me. But pretty soon there's another thing that bothers me, and it's a big thing. Liza is a screamer. It turns out that she is a big fat faker who has just been acting sweet until she's sure Mom and Dad are going to keep her. Right during dinner one night, she has a temper tantrum that's even bigger than the tantrums Jolene's twin Jessie used to have, and Jessie was an expert at tantrums.

I call Andy. "You definitely do not want one of these," I say.

"Why not?"

I hold up the phone, so he can hear why not.

"Oh," he says. "Itzy used to whine, but never anything like that."

"Exactly," I say.

Dad says that maybe they are not tantrums at all. Maybe Liza is just showing her true colors. I see what he means. Baby Liza's true color is red, which is the color her face turns every time she screams.

The doctor says that she has colic, which can't be cured. "You mean she's going to be like this forever?" I say.

"No, it's just something she's going to have to grow out of," my dad says.

There's a good chance I'll be deaf by then. She cries when Mom tries to feed her. She cries when Mom doesn't feed her. She screams when Dad rocks her and when JT walks with her. She yells at anyone who tries to change her diaper. I stay as far away from her as I can. Since we don't know why she starts or what makes her stop—or, when she does stop, when she'll start again—the whole thing is making us all pretty jumpy. The only time I get any quiet at all is during the day, when I go to school. Even lunch in the cafeteria is more relaxing than being in my own house with Loudmouth Liza.

JT can joke about it, but not me. "I guess there's a reason they named her Eliza Ruby—E.R.," he says during one
of her screaming fits. "With her, everything is an emer-
gency."

"Yeah, well, I think the hospital made a mistake," I say.
"About her being a keeper. I think maybe she's a tosser."

"Mary Margaret!" my mom says over Eliza's screaming. "That will be quite enough!"

I go up to my room and make up another poem.

Tiny fingers, tiny toes,
Tiny boogers up your nose.
All you do is cry and poop.
Baby Liza, I hate you.

This time, though, I keep my poem to myself. Because
we are not allowed to say the word *booger* in our house.

Later I ask JT if Mom is pregnant again.

"Not that I know of," he says. "Why?"

"Because she's cranky, just like she was before she had
the baby."

"All that screaming is enough to make anybody cranky,"
JT says. "You can get away from it, but Mom can't. I think
she's just really tired."

Maybe that's why things are starting to show up in
strange places. When I make myself breakfast one morning, I can't find the cold cereal in the cupboard. So I open
up the refrigerator to get yogurt instead, and there's the

cold cereal, right next to the milk. Then I open the microwave so I can warm up a muffin and I find yesterday's mail. I eat three Oreos just to reward myself for getting through making myself breakfast.

JT was right. I am getting away with all kinds of stuff, which is pretty great; but I would rather have my mom. When Baby Liza is crying, Mom carries her. When Liza isn't crying, Mom is busy doing laundry or dishes. Sometimes she'll say, "How are you doing, Loverly?" But when that baby is screaming her head off, Mom can't even hear my answer, which is "Not so good."

I don't get this at all. A pet is too much trouble for my mom, but a baby isn't? I don't know that much about babies or pets. But I think any pet—a fish, an alligator, even a hippopotamus—would not be as much trouble as this baby. And none of them have dander.

Pretty soon, I just can't take it anymore. "I am going on strike," I announce.

"On strike from what?" asks JT.

"On strike from being a member of this family."

"What does that mean?"

"It means I'm getting out of here."

"This I have to see," says JT.

I march up to my mother, who is holding that screaming ball of trouble. I look at Eliza and say, "Oh, shush!" because we are not allowed to say "shut up" at our house. Right then she urps up all over the floor like a little drinking fountain.

Yuck, I think. But at least she stops crying. "Mom," I say. "We have to have a little talk."

"In a minute," she says in her tired voice. While I'm waiting for her, I watch her wipe up Eliza's shirt first, then try to get the spit-up off her own shirt. Her hair needs a good combing, but it looks that way a lot lately. I watch her as, holding Eliza in one arm and a rag in the other, she kneels down to clean up the mess.

Because she has her back to me, I notice the tennis shoes she's wearing, which are pretty beat up. There's a piece of a sticker on the sole, along with some pink stuff that might have been gum once, but it's crusted over now; and along one side there's a coffee stain in the shape of the state of Florida. The shoes look about as saggy as my mom and not that attractive. I'm glad I don't have to wear them. But for a second I put myself in my mother's shoes, and the view from there is not that good. And then I feel a little sorry about the way I've been acting because I know I haven't made it any better for her.

Mom looks up at me. "What is it, Mary Margaret?"

I get down beside her and hold out my hand for the rag. "Can I try?"

She looks at me, then at the rag. "You want to try . . . *this?*"

"Well, yeah."

She hands me the rag. "That would be lovely." She doesn't get up right away. She just rests there for a minute and watches me. "I'm afraid that mopping floors by hand is best suited to the young and flexible—not the old and in-flexible," she says. "Which is also true of having babies, come to think of it."

"You're doing pretty good at it," I say.

"You think so? I'm not too old?"

"No. You're just right."

"I just wish there were more of me to go around. If there were, then maybe you'd like Liza more."

"She's okay," I say, wiping up the last little glop. "If she just wouldn't be so loud."

"She'll grow out of that."

"I wish she'd hurry up. It's like she always has to be the center of attention or something."

"I haven't ever had a baby like *that* before, have I?"

"JT says that I—" And then I stop, because I see that my mom is smiling, all the way up to her eyes, and I get it. "Mo-om! That was a long time ago. I'm not like that anymore."

"I can see that," she says.

Just then the doorbell rings. I jump up and race for the door, because I hear JT on the stairs, trying to beat me to it. He does, just like always. "Some things never change, huh, Mary Margaret?"

It's Marie, the French exchange student who bought one of my Number Two Totes over the summer, and she has two other girls with her. I look all around, but I don't see any dog, even though she's carrying her Number Two Tote. The tote is bulging, so I know there is something in there. To me it looks like there is a LOT of something in there.

Ewwwww. Doesn't she know she's supposed to empty that thing?

"Pardon," she says. She holds out her Number Two Tote. "You have more?"

"Do you have any more of these left?" a girl with long bright red hair asks. "We think they are divine!"

"You do?"

"They are the perfect size for our CDs and our makeup," she says. "We're all just crazy for them!"

Just plain crazy is more like it, I think. "But don't you know what we made them for?" I ask.

The girls all giggle. "Yes," says one. "All this is a little bizarre, but that's okay with us. We have our own sense of style."

"Me, too," I say. "But you still wouldn't catch me—"

JT elbows me in the ribs. "Mary Margaret will run and get them, *won't you*, Mary Margaret?"

And I do. They buy a red velvet one and a leopard-print one. After they leave, I say, "Those girls are nuts! Using Number Two Totes to carry other stuff in! Yuck. Why would they do that?"

"Who cares how they use them?" JT asks, pulling on his tennis shoes. "As long as they're buying them, you're still getting what you want."

"I guess. Where're you going?" I ask.

"Over to the school to practice."

"Practice what?" I hope it's not football! If he's playing football, JT will get squashed, mashed, and mooshed. His whole body will look like his nose did the night Liza was born.

"Not football," he says. "I think I'm going to run cross-country."

"What's cross-country?"

"A long race that you run through fields and woods. Darryl—"

"Duff?"

"He really wants to be called Darryl. Anyway, he's running cross-country because he wants to stay in shape until basketball season, and he said I should try it, too. He said he couldn't believe how fast I caught up to them at the park that night. Anyway, I talked to the coach about joining the team, even though the season has already started. He says I have a runner's build. So I guess I'll give it a shot."

Mom comes out with Liza to wish JT good luck. "You'd better get a sweatshirt," she says. JT rolls his eyes but doesn't bother to argue, just heads inside to get one. Mom holds out her arm to stop him. "Wait!" she says. "Also, take the extra house key because we won't be here when you get back."

"It's still missing, remember?"

"Oh, that's right. I just can't think of where it could be! I know we had it when we got back from vacation last spring," Mom says, frowning. "I can usually find anything, but I haven't been able to find that key."

"Ask Mary Misplaced-It," JT says. "She's the pack rat of the family." And then he disappears into the house.

Pack rat. That makes me wonder about what happened to Lester/Bridgette. Did she have her babies? And why are people who keep everything called pack rats? And that makes me wonder if Lester/Bridgette . . . "Back in a minute!" I say to my mom. I sprint up to my room and dig through the part of my room that Lester holed up in at the beginning of the summer. And there, under a Twinkie wrapper and next to a silver Barbie shoe, is the extra house key. Bridgette must have spent her one night at our house looking for shiny treasures, found the shoe and the key, and carried them back to my room.

I get back to the front porch in time, just as JT is leaving. "Found it!" I say. "Here you go."

"Where was it?" my mom asks.

"In my room, but I didn't put it there. Bridgette did."

"Bridgette?" JT looks puzzled. "You mean the—?"

I nod.

Fortunately, Mom's busy fussing with Liza. "Who's Bridgette?" she asks.

"A friend. She was only here once, and it didn't really work out," I say.

JT says, "Yeah, I remember her. She was kind of mousy-looking." Then he holds out the sweatshirt and the key for Mom to see. "Okay?" he says.

"Okay," she says. "Have a good time."

"Bye, Little Lady," he says.

"My name is Mary Margaret, not Little Lady," I say.

"I was talking to the baby," he says with a grin.

For once, Liza is awake and not crying.

"You want to hold her?" my mom asks.

I've held her before and it's no big deal, really. And maybe Mom's just tired of carrying her around. "All right," I say.

She lays Eliza in my arms so that her head is in the crook of my arm. "Don't forget you have to support her head," she says.

"I know," I say, shifting around to get comfortable. She looks up at me and kind of jerks an arm, like she's saluting me. I almost smile but stop myself. I know what she's up to. She's trying to get me to like her, which someday I probably will. But I don't have to let her know it.

After that, I try to help my mom out a little more. It's not like I'm Little Miss Helper or anything, and I think it will be a while before I try cleaning a toilet again, but sometimes I'll vacuum or fold some clothes. I still can't do it as neatly as Mom, but she doesn't seem to care. She says the only way to learn is by doing it.

I've figured out how I can get some peace and quiet. My dad has a wood-chipping helmet that has special earmuff things attached. They keep out most of the noise when you're chipping wood—or living in a house with a screaming sister. It's bright orange and a little big for me, but it still keeps out the noise. Dad says it may be the start of another fashion trend.

With Liza being her usual loudmouth self, I can see it's

going to be a while before Mom wants to talk about getting a pet again. But a few weeks later, Mom says, "Mary Margaret, let's go for a drive." I don't know everything about babies, but one thing I've learned is that you do *not* want to be stuck in a minivan next to a screaming one—even if you are wearing a wood-chipping helmet.

"No, thanks," I say.

"I guess she wouldn't have to come along," says my dad. Something about the way he says it makes me look up. He has a goofy look on his face.

"You're right," says my mom. "We could pick one out. And it's only fair that I get to pick out the name, since Mary Margaret named the baby."

"Pick out what?" I ask. "Name what?"

My mom puts her finger to her chin and looks at the ceiling. "Let me see. Jake? Leopold? Peter?"

My dad snorts. "Peter would be a good one!"

"What? Where are you going?"

"Hunting rabbits!" my dad says.

"Da-ad," I say. My dad likes to do lots of things, but he doesn't like to hunt. "Stop joking."

"Mary Margaret," Mom says. "Things seem to be getting just a little easier around here for all of us, in part because Liza is settling down a teeny bit. But it's also because everyone—including you—has been helping. So Dad and I think maybe you're ready for a pet. I may not be quite ready, but I'm willing to give it a try."

"Really?"

My dad nods. "We got the idea from what happened at the park the night Eliza was born. We started doing some research on rabbits. Domesticated ones—tame ones—make good pets so—"

"But they have fur," I say, "so they must have dander, too. And that means you're allergic to them."

"Just let me finish," my dad says. "They do have dander, but rabbits can live in a hutch. The man we talked to on the phone said it shouldn't be kept outside because of predators, but we can buy an already-assembled shed for the backyard. He also said that the rabbit would need a lot of attention—you'd need to play with it every day."

"No problem!"

"We know it won't be," says my mom with a laugh.

And that is how I finally get a real pet.

18. Our New Normal

Hershey (which is what I named her because people were always saying "him" and "he" when they talked about her, and then I always had to say "her!" "she!" Plus she is the color of chocolate, so that works pretty well) is sweet (also like chocolate) but not that interesting. She has a collar and a leash, and sometimes I'll take her on a hop around the yard. It takes us about eight hours to get all the way around the yard. Well, maybe not quite that many, but it takes a long time.

When she stops to take a nibble of grass, I usually hang over the fence and watch the pet parade go by. I'd like to be in the parade, too, but I think the dogs would go wild if they saw Hershey. So we stay where it's safe. Besides, Hershey doesn't have that much energy. Mostly she likes to sit quietly in my lap. I wish she were more lively, but Mom and Dad say it's good that she's not. They say it's already a three-ring circus around here.

They are exaggerating. It's been a lot better around

here lately, to tell the truth. Even though Liza still has a temper and lets us know loud and clear when something's wrong, at least now we can usually figure out what it is. I haven't fallen in love with her or anything like that, but I guess that she can stay. We all pitch in so that Mom isn't quite as *exhausted* as she used to be. Dad is the diaper dude, JT is the stroller squad, and I'm the gas girl. I got that job because no one is better at burping Liza than me.

"Ee-yurp," she goes quietly, whenever anyone else burps her. But when I burp her, she really lets it fly. "EEE-YURRRRRRP!"

"Hey," I said to her the first time I got her to do it. "You know what? If you say a little poem after you do that, people smile at you instead of yelling at you. JT taught me that and it really works."

Things never got back to normal, but after a while things started to seem like a new normal, I guess. It's amazing what you can get used to once you're nine. Sometimes I think I'm better at the new normal than my mom. Yesterday when Liza wouldn't stop crying and fussing at my mom, who was trying to do some work on the computer that needed to be done *right then*, she snapped at Liza. "Are you always going to have colic?" she said. "Are you going to act like this in kindergarten? In college?"

"Mom," I said. "Put yourself in her"—I stop to look at Liza's feet—"socks. She's just having a bad day. Everyone is cranky sometimes. You were for a whole nine months." And before my surprised mother could say another word, I put on my wood-chipping helmet and took Liza out to see Hershey.

Liza is part of the new normal. So is JT's not being around much. He's been winning a lot of cross-country races, and when he's not running, he hangs out with some of the other guys on the team. Duff—I mean Darryl—still comes over, but they don't bake cookies anymore. JT says if I want cookies, I'll have to learn to bake them myself. So maybe I will.

Also, girls from middle school keep calling over here, asking when they'll be able to buy Number Two Totes. So I made a deal with Mom. I told her that I'd play with Liza sometimes so she can get her work done if she'll help me make Number Two Totes during Liza's nap. She said, "Change the name to Teen Totes, and I'm in." Then she said that with a little practice I'll probably be able to use the machine all by myself.

Last night my dad took me bowling. (*Bowling?* But I didn't complain. I just went along with it.) He said he needed a night out with his favorite talking daughter, which didn't fool me a bit because I know I'm his only talking daughter. Afterward, he took me to Ben's Belly-Bustin' Burgers for a hamburger and milkshake. He wanted to know if I still have that plan to buy a dog and keep it at the kennel. I do still have that plan. I like Hershey and everything; it's just that I think if I had a dog, my life would be perfect.

"It'll never happen," JT said later.

"What—getting a dog?"

"No, your life being perfect. If it does, you better check your pulse. KWIM?"

"Why?"

"Because if your life is perfect, it probably means you've died and gone to heaven. That's why it'll never happen." But that's just what JT says.

I say you never know. It *could* happen. And for me, I think it just might.